Charity 2

Path of the Pale Horse

A CHARLOTTE ZOLOTOW BOOK

Path of the Pale Horse

Paul Fleischman

1817
HARPER & ROW, PUBLISHERS
Cambridge, Philadelphia, San Francisco, London, Mexico City, São Paulo, Sydney
NEW YORK

First Edition
Designed by Joyce Hopkins
1 2 3 4 5 6 7 8 9 10

Library of Congress Cataloging in Publication Data
Fleischman, Paul.
  Path of the pale horse.

  Summary: Lep, an apprentice to a doctor, helps his
master take care of yellow fever victims in Philadelphia
during the epidemic of 1793.
  [1. Yellow fever—Philadelphia (Pa.), 1793—Fiction.
2. Philadelphia (Pa.)—Fiction] I. Title.
PZ7.F599233Pat 1983   [Fic]   82-48611
ISBN 0-06-021904-1
ISBN 0-06-021905-X (lib. bdg.)

For Anne

Contents

Path of the
Pale Horse

Chapter One

MR. UZZIAH BOTKIN

Among Lep, his mother, and his sister Clara, the name Uzziah Botkin had always been uttered with a hush of reverence reserved, elsewhere in Danfield, for President Washington, selected saints, and Almighty God himself. Each fact of his single, legendary visit, some twenty years earlier, had been gathered up, reliclike, every precious detail worn smooth with repeating: the fire, ignited by a spark from the hearth, that had leveled the silversmith shop of Lep's father, Apollo Nye, four days after opening; Mr. Botkin's detour through Danfield as a result of a washout on the Rumpville road; the passage of his magnificent coach before the rubble, and his call to halt; his peering out the window; his stepping out the door; his plucking from the ashes a silver teapot, raising it, gleaming, up to the light, admir-

3

ing the workmanship in awe; and his generous loan of funds to Lep's father, not to mention the leaving behind of his son, with whom he'd been traveling, to help rebuild the shop. All these had been chiseled into the family memory such that, within the Nye household, the wisdom of Solomon, the patience of Job, the strength of Atlas and Hercules, had been joined by the now-proverbial benevolence of Mr. Botkin.

In five years Lep's father had repaid the loan, in the form of a stream of silver serving trays, sugar bowls, cream pitchers, tankards, and candlesticks shipped the two days' journey east to Mr. Botkin's Philadelphia home. Since then there'd been no word of him, and when the War of Independence claimed Apollo Nye, Lep's mother, left with two infants to raise, had turned to the making of hats and gloves. Clara, fifteen now, still worked alongside her. Lep, a year younger and apprenticed to Dr. Peale, glowed hot, as he always had, with a feverish desire to master medicine and rescue the sick from disease. And although Lep had never set eyes on Mr. Botkin, the man had lived in his thoughts for so long that he was certain he could spot him at once. His hat, he imagined, would be adorned with gold braid. His black velvet coat, ablaze with gold buttons, would glitter as if snipped from the evening sky. He'd stand ceiling-scraping tall. His voice would be deep. And he'd be sure to carry a gold-headed cane, as befitted a man possessing the power to defy fire itself, to refashion lives, and even, Lep had sometimes fancied, to command the very tides and planets.

Therefore, when on one August afternoon in 1793, Lep looked up from Dr. Peale's copy of Cullen's *Materia Medica* to see a gig stop and a man step out who presented himself at the door as Mr. Botkin, he all of a sudden felt strangely faint headed—and was quickly revived by the chance remedy of dropping the bricklike book on his toe.

"Mr.—*Uzziah* Botkin?" Lep stammered.

The man's left eye twitched, as if in reply. "Precisely."

Lep snatched his book off the floor and surveyed the caller in astonishment. He was short legged as a stove, with a soup-kettle belly, and busied himself with chasing the dust from his tattered cuffs and much-mended breeches.

"Step right inside," Lep mumbled, spellbound. "Please, that is," he added. "Sir." He searched in vain for the man's gold-headed cane, gazed in shock at his threadbare coat—whose family of plain pewter buttons had suffered the loss of various members—and breathlessly fetched his mother from the barn.

Mrs. Nye, adjusting her kerchief as she ran, rushed toward the house, bustled inside—and froze, eyeing her guest's ragged dress. "Mr.—Botkin."

He turned. "My *dear* Mrs. Nye."

Lep dashed through the doorway a step before Clara and awaited her reaction. Just because she was a measly year older she acted as if she knew all there was to know and was no longer capable of surprise. Lep smiled, therefore, to find that even she was staring in awe at the visitor, absently clutching her blond braids like two bell ropes.

"You are," Mr. Botkin continued, "the mirror-true image of your former self."

Mrs. Nye, unable to return the phrase, pried her eyes from his battered hat and turned to face her gawking children.

"Heavens afire—are you a pair of stone statues? Clara—there's peaches to be sliced for preserves. Asclepius—bring Mr. Botkin some cider."

Instantly the house filled with commotion. Mrs. Nye pulled a chair away from the table, dusted it with the edge of her apron, and begged her venerable guest to be seated.

"I must confess," Mr. Botkin remarked, "it took me an hour to find the house. And all day to track down this speck of a town."

Mrs. Nye sat down opposite Mr. Botkin and peered pitifully into his drooping eyes, struggling to recognize in him the man she'd seen twenty years earlier.

"Danfield," she apologized, "never was a town to cast much shadow."

Just then Lep approached and, as if serving a monarch, halted stiffly at Mr. Botkin's side.

"Your cider, sir."

Mr. Botkin turned, reached out his right hand to take the mug, and found his gaze fixed, like a compass

6

needle, on the boy's big, molasses-brown eyes. Cow's eyes, Clara jealously called them. Mr. Botkin, his own eye restlessly twitching, proceeded to scrutinize Lep from head to heels, as if considering purchase.

"A fine-looking lad," he addressed Mrs. Nye.

Lep smiled, though he knew he was thin as a wick, and wanted dipping in wax, as his sister liked to say.

"Asclepius," Mrs. Nye replied, "has shown great promise at doctoring." She squirmed in her seat and glanced vaguely out the window. "And what of your own son—who served us so well?"

Mr. Botkin stared into his mug. "My dear Benjamin."

Fearing to be banished outside on some errand, Lep anchored himself within earshot by slicing peaches alongside Clara in the corner—despite the fact it was her chore and not his.

"Benjamin," Mr. Botkin lamented, "left Pennsylvania for the Ohio country, in search of the fortune he deserved to inherit. This, it grieves me to say, the result of a string of reverses that humbled the once-mighty merchant firm of Botkin and Hyde."

Mr. Botkin contemplated his cider, then drank it down quickly, as if it were a longed-for dose of hemlock.

"Great quakes, Mrs. Nye, and mighty winds and waves have assailed my fortunes since first we met. A fact you've no doubt been alerted to by the present state of my dress."

"Not at all!" Mrs. Nye, her heart full and her fingers trembling, abruptly averted her eyes from the man.

"Alas, the force of the calamity was felt by many besides myself. Dear Judith, my wife, overwhelmed by the change, lay down to die that very December. My son soon fled west, my servants were dismissed. And last winter my youngest brother, Ulysses, whose failures in numerous ventures in the past had left him dependent on my charity, grew weak on what little food I could spare him, took ill, and was buried in the family plot."

Lep's hands had gradually slowed to a halt. Blankly, he gazed at the cutting board, until all of a sudden Clara delivered a kick to his ankle and he resumed his slicing.

"Forgive me for troubling you with my trials." Mr. Botkin stared at the floor and sighed. Then he raised his eyes, spied the pair of silver candlesticks on the mantel, and smiled. "And kindly excuse my calling him from his undoubtedly profitable enterprise, but might I speak with Mr. Nye?"

Clara's own knife ceased striking the board.

"I'm afraid Mr. Nye is no more," said Lep's mother. "Cut down during the war, he was."

Mr. Botkin's mouth dropped open in awe.

"Since then the enterprise, such as it is, has been the sewing of hats and gloves."

Mr. Botkin swallowed and shuffled his feet. His eye twitched nervously. "I see." His vision of a thriving silversmith shop, tended by a prosperous Mr. Nye, quickly melted away.

"Perhaps then," he murmured, as if to himself, "my journey might better have not been made." He glanced haphazardly about the room, noticed a table covered with scraps of calfskin and velvet, and released a sigh.

"Having recently found myself face to face with an extraordinary commercial opportunity—whose details I'm not at liberty to divulge, yet which promises to restore my lost fortune in full—I conceived the notion of traveling to York, hiring a gig, and seeking out Mr. Nye." Mr. Botkin, hesitating, cleared his throat. "In hopes of arranging—for a modest loan."

Lep started. The sound of Clara's knife ceased once more.

Mrs. Nye shifted anxiously in her seat.

"Great fortunes," she faltered, "as you surely know, aren't built from kid gloves and summer bonnets."

She licked her lips and inhaled deeply. "And what few works of silver Mr. Nye left I've drawn on only in cases of the greatest need."

She smoothed the wrinkles out of her apron. Then she lifted her eyes to Mr. Botkin's creased features— and was overwhelmed with pity for the man.

"And this," she announced with sudden resolution, "must be considered as just such a case."

Lep smiled and watched his mother rise and reach for the candlesticks on the mantel.

"I believe you'll find that the silver amounts to

twenty-five dollars apiece, at the least." She set them down before Mr. Botkin. "I only wish I could offer you more."

The polished candlesticks glinted proudly, as if striving to show they could light a room with no help from the stubby wax candles they bore. Mr. Botkin, struck speechless, handled one, then the other, gazing upon them in rapture.

"I give you my word on the matter, Mrs. Nye, that this undertaking can't fail of success. You may expect to receive, indeed *rely* on, full repayment in three months' time."

"I'm afraid I shall have to," Mrs. Nye replied. "Dr. Peale's fee for Lep's apprenticeship will be due the first of December."

Lep realized he'd forgotten this fact. A serving tray and a pair of tankards had paid for his first year of training, he recalled, and he focused his eyes on the candlesticks with a sudden air of concern.

"Three months," Mr. Botkin proclaimed. "Have no fear."

He cleared his throat several times. "However," he added, "the success of this astounding opportunity would be absolutely and utterly *assured* were I given an able assistant." Mr. Botkin cast his eyes toward Lep. "As my Benjamin served, without payment, when called on."

Lep looked up to meet Mr. Botkin's gaze, put down

his knife, and faced his mother, panic-stricken by this threat to his studies.

"We are grateful, naturally," Mrs. Nye fumbled, "*exceedingly* grateful for Benjamin's help."

Mr. Botkin slid his chair closer to hers. "A mere three months' term would be more than sufficient."

Mrs. Nye produced a handkerchief and dabbed desperately at her brow. "Lep, I'm afraid, is serving as Dr. Peale's assistant—here in Danfield."

Lep crossed the room and stood beside her. Smiling, she put her hand on his shoulder, proud to have protected him. Then she noted Mr. Botkin's long-suffering shoes—and shuddered to think of her situation had he not been so free with his own charity.

"I'm sorry," she said. "I do wish I could help."

Glumly, Mr. Botkin studied the floor. Then his eye commenced twitching.

"What about the girl?"

Clara felt a chill of excitement climb her spine. She set down her knife, her eyes wide as gold dollars.

"My daughter?" Mrs. Nye glanced worriedly at the girl, trying the notion on for fit like one of her own kid gloves.

"Of course, Clara helps with the sewing," she put forward, searching her wits for a stouter objection. "Nimble with a needle, she is."

Mr. Botkin, eyes squinting, palms propped on his knees, assessed the girl across the length of the room.

"Then again," Clara piped up cautiously, "Mrs. Wigglesworth's four pairs of gloves have been finished."

She hoped that her mother didn't think her disloyal. But a chance to see Philadelphia, she knew, might never pass within reach again.

"And we've not had a new order since," she added. With seeming indifference she returned to her slicing, while her whirling mind conjured up scenes of the bustling Philadelphia streets and the fabled three-block-long market she'd heard of from a peddler.

"Naturally," Mr. Botkin announced, "I shall gladly furnish her meals and lodging. And when the venture's blossoms bear their fruit, I shall insist on paying her stage fare back home."

All at once Lep felt acutely aware of the fact that he'd never seen Philadelphia himself. Shamefaced, he reflected that he'd never even crossed the Susquehanna River, twenty-five miles to the east—and for an instant he regretted his medical studies, wishing he were free to accompany Mr. Botkin. As it was, Clara carried on as though her experience were incomparably vaster than his own. But once she'd seen the nation's capital, there'd be no hope of getting the importance out of her.

"They've got water brought right into some of the houses *with pipes*," Clara informed her mother. "And a garden with every known plant in the world. And all manner of modern, scientific advancements we can hardly imagine in a place like Danfield."

Lep gazed sourly at his sister. She'd buy wooden nutmegs by the bushel, he mused, if she was told they were a modern, scientific improvement on the original.

Mrs. Nye viewed her daughter. "You're only fifteen—"

Clara struggled to mask her indignation. "And if I were so much as a single year younger," she politely replied, glancing at Lep, "I fear I'd not benefit fully from exposure to the great city on the Hudson."

Mr. Botkin smiled. "No doubt you're thinking of the Delaware."

Lep grinned triumphantly back at his sister.

"Yes—of course," Clara sputtered. She turned toward her mother. "And we're fully caught up on our hats," she added emphatically, struggling to bury her error.

Lep's mother touched her handkerchief to her brow. "I suppose it's a fact that customers have been awfully scarce this week." She looked out the window and down the road. "Not a thing's come in through the door except flies."

She clasped her hands. "Well now, Clara. You're certain that you want to go?"

"I should be proud to," Clara replied. "To fulfill my duty to serve when called on—as Mr. Botkin's Benjamin did."

Lep's mother sighed. Then she smiled weakly. "I expect your father would have wished it so."

Clara's eyes lit up. Mr. Botkin beamed.

"At the moment, however," Mrs. Nye declared, "your *duty* is to start supper—for four, of course."

Mr. Botkin smiled. "How I wish there were time. As it happens, however, the stage that I've arranged passage on leaves York this evening. I'm afraid we haven't a moment to spare."

Bursting into action as if she'd swallowed ball lightning, Clara frantically packed her clothes while Lep, feeling distinctly left out, found paper, pen, and ink for Mr. Botkin.

"Here's the address," he informed Mrs. Nye, handing her the piece of paper. "Far from the luxury I was accustomed to once, but clean and respectable, I assure you."

Clara reappeared, a pink bonnet on her head and her father's trunk in her arms.

"Well now." Lep's mother straightened Clara's bonnet. "Things have taken to happening so fast."

They all walked outside. Lep took the trunk and placed it on the floor of the gig.

"No time to lose," Mr. Botkin warned.

Clara turned and kissed her mother. She smiled, a trifle smugly, at Lep. She climbed up, and Mr. Botkin snapped the reins. And suddenly they were off down the road.

That night, after cleaning the supper dishes, a chore his sister had always performed, Lep lit a lamp, climbed into bed, reopened the well-worn leather cover of Cullen's *Materia Medica*—and instantly forgot that he wasn't bound for Philadelphia instead.

He returned to poring over the chapter devoted to stimulants. Their powers to increase the mobility of fluids, their effects on the blood, the stomach, the senses—all these Lep committed to memory as if his life depended on it.

His mother called out her good night to him; he answered without raising his eyes from the page. Soon after, he noticed that she'd blown out her lamp. Lep read on, as he did every night.

The uses of hyssop's essential oils; lavender's powers in the treatment of palsy; marjoram, sage, infusions of mint; the virtues of rosemary, anise, angelica.

Fighting to keep his eyelids open, Lep yawned and considered closing the book. Then he looked out the window beside his bed, chanced to glimpse a falling star—and at once sat up and returned to his reading, his mind suddenly sharp as a lancet. For a falling star, his mother had told him, had been seen by Mrs. Weeks, the midwife, on her way to attend to Lep's own birth. And this omen of loss had been fulfilled that same night when a letter was handed Lep's grandfather, pacing outside his daughter's door, describing the death of Apollo Nye in the battle of Stony Point, in New York, and his whispered final request, "A doctor . . ."

Lep lifted his eyes from the page a moment. He imagined he heard the tramp of armies, the crack of muskets. And the cries of the wounded . . .

That night, when Lep's mother had asked her father inside to see the newborn child, he'd mentioned nothing at all of the letter. And when she'd sought his advice on the choice of a name, he'd recalled the ancient mythology he'd taught in his years as a schoolmaster, and offered her "Asclepius."

"A son of Apollo," he'd murmured, explaining.

"Truly now—how appropriate. And what was this Asclepius besides?"

Her father had sighed, squeezing the letter in the pocket of his coat. "A doctor."

Lep's mother had smiled and admired her son's eyes.

"A doctor of extraordinary powers. Among them, even the power—or so it was said—of bringing the dead back to life."

Chapter Two

TO THE RESCUE

At first light Lep was already dressed and finished with a bowl of corn mush and cream. He fed the chickens. He milked the cow. Then he tucked the *Materia Medica* under his arm and set off for Dr. Peale's.

It was a two-mile walk. The sun, just rising, shimmered at the end of the road and Lep strode along toward it as purposefully as if it were his destination. He passed Judge Pike's and surveyed his parched cornfield. Raindrops had been scarce as rubies that summer. Streams had withered in the August heat and the roads were choked with dust. Kicking up a cloud as he went, Lep finally squeezed through a break in a hedge and entered a cramped stone house.

"*Salvete!*" Dr. Peale called out, seated at his desk and scanning Lep's Latin lesson of the day before. He removed his spectacles from his bony nose. *"Discipulus bonus habeo,"* he added, signifying that he had an excellent pupil.

"Magister bonus habeo," replied Lep, indicating that he had an excellent teacher.

Dr. Peale, convinced that vanity was the most lethal of the seven deadly sins, steeled himself against this compliment and returned his eyes to Lep's exercises. Replacing the *Materia Medica* on its shelf, Lep reached for a broom and swept the floors. Then he marched outside to attend to the herb garden while Dr. Peale hummed and whistled by turns—until suddenly he fell silent. All at once he shot to his feet, quickly covered the length of the room in three great strides of his heronlike legs, and brought down the toe of his shoe on a beetle.

"Vile creature," he muttered to himself, staring accusingly at the insect whose kind had led him into vanity's clutches. Studying the beetle, he tortured himself with the memory of his return to Philadelphia at the close of his medical studies abroad. Seduced by the promise of fame in the sciences, he'd enlisted an English schoolmate of his—a lifelong student of insect ways—in a walking trip certain to turn up a trove of unrecorded species. But just north of the city they'd approached a meadow—a meadow in which Dr. Peale remembered once seeing scores of emerald-green beetles. Trembling with visions of being first to describe them and naming the species after himself, he'd proposed that his friend strike out toward the west, which he did—and where, while exploring a slope, his companion slipped, struck his head on a rock, and suffered a blow to his brain that left him able only to babble like an infant.

Acidly, Dr. Peale eyed the bug, wishing he could rid the world of beetles, whose endless multiplication was to have kept the flame of his fame alive. Shuddering at the thought of his folly, he glanced gratefully at his powders and potions and returned to his work, reinvigorated. The practice of medicine, he'd found, was a potent cure for inflamed pride, and the day after his schoolmate had sailed for home, he'd packed his belongings, left Philadelphia, where vanity reigned supreme, and settled in Danfield, far removed from temptation, devoting his life to the service of others.

Lep strode inside. "The garden's watered."

"And how is the yarrow faring, Lep?"

"Thriving again, sir. And nearly ready for harvest."

Dr. Peale regarded the boy with wonder. "You've a way with the plants, Lep. I do believe you could coax a mayapple into bloom in December."

He stood up and studied his shelves of medicines. "Now then. This morning you'll need to grind cloves. And we're quite low on catmint leaves as well."

Lep sprang into action, seized mortar and pestle, and commenced to grind as vigorously as if the entire world were lined up outside, crying out for clove powder.

"We're in need of syrup of violets also," continued Dr. Peale. He gazed upon his busy apprentice, delighting in the sound of mortar and pestle as if it were the music of the spheres. Mixing medicines, healing the ill—this was a laudable life, he mused. Then, horrified, he realized that such self-satisfaction was vanity's snare—and sternly rededicated himself to subduing the beast of pride within.

To this end he dressed plainly. He would wear no wigs, and tied back his fair hair with a tattered black ribbon. As an expression of humility, he'd constructed his house low to the ground—so low, he'd acquired a permanent stoop—and hidden it from the road with a hedge, lest he seem to be striving to attract attention. Likewise, he refused to let Lep call him "Master"; parried all praise that came his way, as if deflecting swords thrust at his heart; and when finding the still-living embers of pride, quickly submerged himself in his work.

Desperately, he opened his account book and plunged into the study of his finances. "And Lep—we have need of more rhubarb."

"Yes, sir."

Dr. Peale contemplated the crushed beetle. "And more humility, as always."

Lep girded himself against vanity. "Yes, sir."

He ground. He grated. He boiled. He strained. All morning long he bustled about, then embarked outdoors on a collecting trip. After picking what he could from the herb garden, he roamed the woods and fields nearby, harvesting flowers and berries and barks, knowing just where to find what he needed. Other people, he knew, feared Nature, but for him the countryside was an ally, a great medicine chest whose contents offered cures for every known affliction.

After returning, Lep did various chores for which Dr. Peale had reduced his fee. He split firewood and raised water from the well, trimmed the lamps and refilled them with oil. Then he studied another lesson in Latin, after which Dr. Peale announced that they'd be setting off on a round of visits.

Lep walked to the barn. "Come on, Hitabel."

Dr. Peale's ash-gray mare lifted her ears.

"That's right. We're going out for a spell." He slipped on the halter, led her outside, hitched her to the gig, and fed her some hay. She was nervous by nature and easily spooked, but she'd come to trust Lep, who stood stroking her nose. Dr. Peale, medicine chest in hand, then walked out the door and headed for the gig, making a slight detour to lower his shoe, vengefully, on a beetle.

"Mr. Say's wife stopped by last night." Dr. Peale climbed up and shook the reins. "It sounds like he may have a throat distemper."

They passed the church and the White Raven inn and halted before a stately brick house. Mrs. Say, stout as a flour barrel and attired in a gold satin gown, led them inside to her husband's bed.

"It's worsened up since last night," she declared. Her hands fluttered about like caged birds. "Fever's come into it—his head's like a griddle!" She pulled out a handkerchief and mopped her own brow.

"Fever, you say." Dr. Peale viewed her gown, wincing at the vanity radiating from such richness of dress.

"A slight warmth—nothing more," Mr. Say spoke up hoarsely.

"But those chills!" Mrs. Say shivered a moment herself. "And that pain—at the very base of the throat." She indicated the site on her own anatomy.

"I see," responded Dr. Peale, wondering which of the parties to treat. Turning, he studied Mr. Say's plump face, round as a full moon rising out of the sheets.

"Lep—kindly take Mr. Say's pulse."

Lep opened his father's silver pocket watch and reached for the patient's wrist.

"Ninety-six strokes a minute," he reported.

"Well now." Dr. Peale peered down the man's throat, then put his hand on Mr. Say's forehead, humming, then whistling, then humming again, as if he were a one-man antiphonal choir.

"Yes indeed—a slight fever. Bleeding will help. Sixteen ounces should be sufficient." He opened up his medicine chest and handed his apprentice a lancet. "Lep here will perform the task while I prepare a pill for your throat."

"Him?" Mr. Say burst out. "He's but a boy!"

"And quite able, I assure you," replied Dr. Peale.

Glad to take the offensive against illness, Lep made three careful cuts in Mr. Say's upper arm, watched closely by his wary patient, and filled his bowl to the sixteen-ounce line. Dr. Peale, observing him bandage the arm, noted the departure of Mr. Say's suspicion. Lep's eyes inspired trust, he reflected—he'd seen it happen time and again. And his confidence in his cures was contagious.

"Excellent, Lep. Now if Mr. Say will take this." He handed the patient a calomel pill. "After which, this gargle of tincture of aloes and myrrh should offer some modest relief."

He held out a cup to Mr. Say, who dutifully began to gargle.

"We'd hoped that Turlington's Balsam of Life might heal him," Mrs. Say piped up. "But alas—we discovered the bottle was empty."

"And just as well." Dr. Peale stared silently at the woman. "The miracle mongers who take money for such potions stand with war, famine, storm, and the rest of mankind's greatest enemies."

Lep spotted the empty bottle on a table and eyed it contemptuously. Quickly he packed up the medicine chest while Dr. Peale, accepting his payment, noted with distaste Mrs. Say's brocade slippers and led the way out the door.

Climbing into the gig, they set off down the road, pressing the attack on disease in cases of colic, toothache, and inveterate itch before returning home. Having pulled his first tooth, with Dr. Peale's brass tooth key, Lep glowed with a sense of accomplishment while he unhitched Hitabel, led her to the barn, brushed her, and headed homeward himself.

The sun was low and shadows long, as if they meant to sneak off from their owners. A fine coach passed Lep by, maroon with gold trim. A cloud of blackbirds swooped through the sky. Lep looked at the *Materia Medica* and figured out on what day he'd be finished, anxious to begin bringing home Haller's *Physiology*.

He opened the book and tried reading while he walked. Then he raised his eyes while rounding a bend and spotted the coach that had passed him earlier— leaning, a wheel sunk in a pothole, and one man kneeling over another on the ground.

Lep sprinted down the road to the coach.

"Is he hurt?"

The kneeling man whirled about. "Marcus—my footman! Thrown from his seat!" The speaker was shaking and oblivious of the dirt he was getting on his elegant attire. "Do you think—like poor Edmund— do you suppose that he's—dead?"

"Dead?"

The footman's eyes opened briefly. He was burly and red-faced, with a twisted upper lip. Hurriedly, Lep examined him.

"No broken bones. He seems just to be dazed." Lep plucked a handkerchief out of his pocket and pressed it to a gash above the footman's hairline. "No doubt from the knock he took to his head."

The gentleman's tufted gray eyebrows shot up. "Merely dazed—do you think it possible?" He beamed like a prisoner reprieved from the gallows, gazing at Lep as upon his deliverer. Then suddenly his features darkened. He gripped Lep's arm with his trembling fingers and fixed upon him an owllike stare.

"But tell me now, lad—did your ears make out thunder?"

"*Thunder?*" Lep scanned the cloudless sky.

"Just at the moment that Marcus fell!"

Lep stared at the man in disbelief and noticed a short scar on the tip of his chin. "No, sir. Not a bit of thunder at all."

Lep studied the footman, then looked about and spied a sassafras tree down the road. "Hold the handkerchief to the wound," he instructed. Marcus began squirming. "I'll be back in a moment."

He rushed toward the tree, opened his knife, and dug through the ground to get at the roots. Sassafras roots, he knew, held great powers—especially with ailments involving the head. He cut two small strips and sliced them up finely. Then glancing about, his eyes leaped at the sight of a pair of angelica plants nearby. Quick as a cat he pounced upon them, plucked their leaves, and pressed out their juice. This, he recalled, would relieve inflammation, and he mixed it with the sassafras root and flew back down the road to the coach.

"Blasted country cowpaths," murmured Marcus.

"Let me tend to him," Lep urgently offered. Taking the footman's head in his arms, he succeeded in stopping the flow of blood, cleaned the wound, applied his concoction, and held it in place by rolling the handkerchief and tying it around the man's head.

"Do you think that will help?"

"Yes, sir. Most surely."

The gentlemen peered at Lep in awe, as if beholding an angel from heaven. Slowly, he stood up, large limbed and square shouldered. "I am much—very much—in your debt," he stammered. "William Tweakfield's my name. Retired, from the law. And to whom do I owe my gratitude?"

"Lep Nye, sir." Preoccupied with his patient, he cleaned the dirt from the footman's face. "Apprentice to Dr. Alexander Peale."

Marcus raised himself up on his elbows.

"Damnable potholes!" the footman swore. He reached for his head and grimaced in pain. "And what's this, then?" he asked, feeling the handkerchief.

"A bandage," Mr. Tweakfield answered. "Most ably applied by young Lep here."

Marcus glanced at the apprentice suspiciously. Rising up, he staggered down the road, stretching his legs and regaining his senses.

"Great blazing comets," Mr. Tweakfield muttered. He shook his head. "A miracle!"

"Merely a knock on the head," countered Lep.

"A mere knock!" Mr. Tweakfield grasped Lep's arm. "It was just such a knock that killed poor Edmund, my faithful footman of twenty-two years." His heavy eyebrows lowered like stormclouds. "Just last summer—on this identical route. We were returning to Philadelphia from the solitude of my sister's home, when a great wind came up and a tree branch came down, striking the horses, who panicked and ran the coach off the road—causing Edmund to be thrown." Mr. Tweakfield sighed. "And now young Marcus. I feel as I did back during the war, seeing my men felled one by one."

Lep pricked up his ears. "In which battles did you serve?"

"Trenton, Brandywine, Germantown, Stony Point—"

Lep started. "My father fought at Stony Point!"

Mr. Tweakfield's eyes lit. "Truly now. And what was his name?"

"Apollo Nye."

Mr. Tweakfield searched his memory. "I'm afraid I don't recollect the name."

"But you were actually there," the apprentice mumbled.

"And not likely to forget it either." Mr. Tweakfield fingered the scar on his chin. "Had a musket ball graze me," he added absently.

Lep gazed upon the man, entranced, and seemed to hear the tramp of boots, the booming of guns, and the whizzing of bullets. "And you yourself?" he suddenly cried out. "Are you hurt?" He peered into Mr. Tweakfield's eyes, desperate to offer some aid.

"Not at all." He removed his black beaver hat. "Beyond a slight dent in the brim here, that is."

"You're certain?" Lep was flooded with a sudden feeling of attachment to the man.

"Not so much as a scratch, I assure you."

The sounds of battle faded from Lep's ears. Looking up, he saw Marcus approach, glare at the coach, and kick the sunken wheel.

"These blasted roads be rough enough to shake loose the teeth from a mountain goat." His lip curled upward like a snarling dog's. Then he bent down, grabbed hold of the wheel, and with a mighty effort raised it from the hole. The matched pair of white horses hitched to the coach nervously shifted their feet.

"Well done, Marcus," declared Mr. Tweakfield. "Any damage to report?"

"Just two cracked spokes."

Here, Lep thought, was the sound that Mr. Tweakfield had taken for thunder. Yet when he turned around toward the man, he found him worriedly scanning the sky, as if still searching for the phantom storm.

"And one cracked skull," continued Marcus. He touched his hand to his forehead and winced. "Tree branches, potholes, hailstorms, hornets—if these be the joys of the footman's life, I believe I might seek out some other employment." He beat the dust out of his hat. "Something more suited to a man of my tastes. Like dressing up fine and riding *in* coaches, instead of holding the reins."

He climbed up on his perch. Mr. Tweakfield approached Lep.

"You can't know—what your aid has meant," he faltered. "Simply name your fee and it shall be yours."

Lep appeared shocked at the notion. "Not a penny, sir." And had he the chance, he thought to himself, he'd have attended to Mr. Tweakfield as well, all day and all night, in the rain, for no charge.

"Come now." Mr. Tweakfield reached into a pocket and produced a gold dollar. "I insist."

Lep gaped at the coin, and couldn't help thinking of all the medical books it could buy.

"I'm afraid I couldn't, sir—I'm just an apprentice. And it wasn't any trouble at all."

Mr. Tweakfield frowned. "Very well, Lep."

He climbed into the coach, then stuck his head out the door. "But at least allow me to offer you my grateful hospitality, should you ever set foot in Philadelphia. My house is at the corner of Mulberry and Sixth streets. I shall look forward to finding you on the doorstep someday."

Lep smiled at the man. "Thank you, sir."

Marcus furiously snapped his whip and cursed the horses into action. The coach bolted forward and diminished down the road. Lep watched it disappear, then continued homeward and spied his mother in the garden. He hurried, anxious to tell her about Mr. Tweakfield, but held his tongue when he saw her expression.

"What's happened?" he asked.

She put down her basket.

"I'm concerned for poor Clara." She wiped her hands on her apron. "A peddler came by this afternoon— he'd set out from Philadelphia a week ago. He said that the town was all astir. Due to some sailors—found dead. Of yellow fever."

Chapter Three

NO. 8, ELBOW LANE

Gradually bits of news of the fever were deposited in Danfield, borne along the roads like burrs riding the hides of various travelers. A bookseller stopping the night at the White Raven left a Philadelphia newspaper that advised bathing in vinegar to ward off the disease. The postrider brought Mr. Say a letter that complained of the constant tolling of church bells due to the increase in funerals. A tinker passing through reported that people were fleeing the city for their lives—and that some of the outlying towns wouldn't take them. Troops, it was said, had been called upon to bar the road to Baltimore, for fear the infection should spread to that city. Soon the Philadelphia stages stopped running. And news of dire omens trickled in: Lightning had flashed out of a clear sky in Kensington;

a plague of mosquitoes had attacked Philadelphia; and there, on September twelfth, in the morning, a meteorite had fallen on Third Street.

Lep's mother had at once written Clara a letter crammed with questions as to her safety. Day after day she busied her fingers with a sudden rash of orders for gloves, anxiously awaiting an answer.

The swallows left. The leaves began falling. October arrived, yet there was still no reply.

One afternoon she looked up from her work to find Dr. Peale's gig approaching. She opened the front door just as Lep stepped down.

"Mrs. Nye, good day," said Dr. Peale. "I wished to stop by to inform you that, due to the halting of the stage, I've begun to run low on various drugs normally shipped by my apothecary." Dr. Peale paused. "I'm afraid that my duty commands that I travel to Philadelphia."

Lep spun about, having heard nothing of this.

His mother's face paled. "Philadelphia?"

"I've made up my mind to depart tomorrow." Dr. Peale cast a glance at his apprentice. "And I should like Lep to come with me."

Lep stiffened in astonishment.

"But the fever!" Mrs. Nye reached out for Lep's shoulder.

"We shan't dawdle in the city—have no fear. On the contrary, we'll attend to our task and turn back toward Danfield straight away, with hardly enough time to take in a breath of Philadelphia air."

Mrs. Nye viewed her son. "But why do you need Lep?"

"Due to the drought, the roads—so I've heard—are two feet deep in dust in places. Wagon wheels have sunk to their axles. Thus, besides the comfort of his company, I may need to rely on his arms to help push."

"I see," mumbled Lep's mother, her mind miles away. Suddenly she blinked, as if waking from a trance. "By all means—and Godspeed!"

Lep gaped, amazed.

"Provided you'll execute one further errand."

Desperately, she peered up at Dr. Peale. "Seek out Lep's sister—and bring her back home."

Lep started.

"It's six weeks now with no letter from her. I can scarcely thread a needle from worrying." Mrs. Nye wrung her hands and turned toward Lep. "She's only served half her three months, I know. And I hate to go back on my work to Mr. Botkin. Tell him he can repay the money when he likes—just fetch Clara back again, alive!"

Lep's eyes widened. "But the apprenticeship fee!"

"Business has breezed up of late," said his mother. "We'll manage. Just come back home safe with Clara."

Dr. Peale cleared his throat. "You may count upon it." He eyed his apprentice. "Be ready by cock holler."

Lep was ready. Two hours before sunrise he was

sitting outside by the door, in the blackness, listening to the cryptic conversation of the owls. At last Dr. Peale drove up in his gig. Weighted down with two apple pies, a jug of cider, and three loaves of bread, Lep climbed aboard and Dr. Peale snapped the reins. They were off for Philadelphia.

"I'd hoped never again to set eyes on my native city," Dr. Peale declared.

"Yes, sir," said Lep, though he himself was fit to burst with excitement at the prospect. Armored with his knowledge of medicine, he scoffed at the fear of the fever held by others and even looked forward to glimpsing this ancient enemy face to face.

"I should never choose the mighty Delaware River," Dr. Peale proclaimed, "over our own Hickory Creek."

"No, sir."

Dr. Peale paused. "But in this case, duty demands that we go."

"Yes, sir," Lep was quick to agree.

Shortly, the sun presented itself, glittering like a great gold doubloon.

"We'll stay the night at the Sheaves," said Dr. Peale, "and reach Philadelphia the next afternoon."

Lep opened a paper with Mr. Botkin's address, then tucked it deep into his pocket again.

"At once," continued Dr. Peale, "we'll purchase a fresh supply of camphor, plus quicksilver, opium, and Peruvian bark. Then we'll squeeze in Clara, depart by dusk, and arrive back late the following night."

Lep nodded and watched the road unwind. The sky brightened. The day heated up, and Lep shed his black coat and rolled up his sleeves. At noon they stopped and ate one of the pies. An hour later they reached the banks of the majestic Susquehanna River.

"Going *east?*" inquired a snake-armed ferryman. He pulled a long-stemmed pipe from his mouth and studied the pair quizzically.

"East," replied Dr. Peale distinctly, and led Hitabel aboard the ferry. Frightened, she swung her head about. Quickly, Lep hopped down to calm her while the ferryman pushed off with his pole.

"Most folks be headed *west,*" he remarked, as if his customers might change their minds. "Ahead of the Lord-sent pestilence."

Hardly hearing, Lep gazed at the vastness of the river, dazzled to be crossing it in any direction. Feeling all that was familiar receding, his mind swirled with imaginings of the mysteries beyond the eastern bank.

It was nearly an hour before they landed. Dr. Peale held out three coins in his palm, which the ferryman had him drop one by one into a jar of vinegar.

"I know you're not coming from Philadelphia," the ferryman apologized. He glanced at the jar, half full of coins. "But a body can't be too careful, I say."

Lep curled his nose at a whiff of the vinegar. Dr. Peale flicked the reins and the gig rumbled forward, past farms that Lep was surprised to find looked the same as those in Danfield.

"I do not intend to allow this jaunt to detract from your studies, Lep. Not for a moment." Dr. Peale produced a Latin primer and noted the sun. *"Horae fugiunt."*

"The hours flee," Lep translated to himself, and set to studying while light remained. When he could no longer make out the words on the page, he closed his book and looked up to see a large stone house from which hung a sign.

"Well now—our lodging," beamed Dr. Peale. He stretched his long neck, peering at the sign upon which were painted three golden sheaves. "Said to be among the best to be had."

He drew to a halt before the inn. In the door stood a red-faced woman with a broom, chasing a cloud of dust outside.

"And what is it *you* want?" she addressed Dr. Peale.

"Why, a meal, and a mattress if you've any to spare."

The woman swiped at a deerfly with her broom. "And I *suppose* you be bound for Philadelphia."

Dr. Peale cocked his head. "Yes, that's right."

"And I *suppose* you be a pair of doctors as well!"

Dr. Peale appeared puzzled. "Indeed we are, madam."

At that the woman flung out a laugh. "My, how the doctors have multiplied lately! Thick as the locusts in Egypt, they are." She leveled a knowing eye at Dr. Peale. "Do you take me for a thimblewit? You be no more doctors than the *last* ones who tried it—scampering east to escape the plague and circling around on the Ryebury road so's to seem to be going *toward* Philadelphia. Hoping I'd let you in that way—along with the infection!"

"But madam—"

The woman picked up a handful of stones. "Doctors! Flocking to the call of duty!" She let fly the stones, striking Hitabel's legs. The horse neighed and reared up. "Now be off!"

Dr. Peale grasped the reins, gave them a shake, and the horse charged forward down the road.

For another hour they drove through the darkness without catching sight of a single light, and at last halted for the night in a meadow. Early in the morning they were off again, watching as the clouds caught fire like tinder torched by the rising sun.

"Well, Lep," Dr. Peale spoke up. "Today you'll be given an opportunity to sharpen your powers of diagnosis."

Lep glanced at his mentor and found him staring off in the distance like a statued general.

"You will encounter a seemingly healthy city, adorned with fine buildings, bustling with commerce, frenzied with activity. A city renowned for its brilliant achievements and chosen the nation's capital, a place whose people sport every refinement and attire themselves in the latest fashions."

37

His heart racing, Lep leaned forward in his seat, hoping a view of their destination might appear around the next bend.

"In truth," retorted Dr. Peale, "the color in its cheeks is but the fever of pride. Its rapid pulse—the mad pursuit of fame and riches by its citizens." Icily, he gazed ahead, imagining Philadelphia's corpse laid out before him for autopsy. "A city mortally diseased, it is, Lep—covered with the pockmarks and boils of vanity."

"Yes, sir," Lep replied, hoping that his excitement had gone undetected.

At noon they stopped to rest Hitabel, then pushed on, encountering more and more travelers headed the other way. On foot and on horseback, riding wagons and carts, they raised a gritty veil of dust, behind which they passed like faces in a dream. Finally, they crossed the Schuylkill River. By the time they entered Philadelphia it was dusk.

"Well now," Dr. Peale sighed. "At last."

Dismayed, Lep cast his eyes about. Most shops were closed, many houses shuttered. The brick-paved sidewalks were nearly deserted. A midwinter stillness hung over the street, and it seemed to Lep that the sound of their wheels might carry to every corner of the city.

"Naturally—under normal conditions," Dr. Peale faltered, himself unnerved, "the town presents a far different picture."

Lep gaped, astonished that this could be the mighty metropolis he'd heard of. He beheld the work of the fever in awe, finding his earlier cockiness gone and fighting off his fear by reminding himself that the superior powers of medicine would soon, no doubt, drive out the disease.

A shot rang out a few blocks away. Hitabel's ears flew up at once and she spurted forward in fear.

"Discharging muskets to cleanse the air." Dr. Peale struggled to rein in his horse. "With the shortage of lightning and rain this summer, many believe the ether to be foul and in need of purification."

Curiously, Lep stared at the sky.

"Some say it may even have spawned the fever."

They continued on in the dying light, nearly colliding with a funeral procession consisting of a black man, a cart with a coffin, and a pair of women at a safe distance to the rear, clutching bags of camphor to their noses. Turning down an alleyway, they passed before a bonfire intended to consume the contagion in the air. In the middle of the following block they halted.

"I shan't be a moment fetching our supplies." Dr. Peale handed the reins to Lep. "You'd best stay here with Hitabel."

He stepped down, strode past a water pump, and tried the door to a shop. It was locked. He rapped with a shiny door knocker, cast in the shape of a pestle, and waited. He knocked again, more loudly this time. Ducking under the apothecary's sign, he peered through a window, then walked toward the rear. Lep heard a knock. A door opened, then banged shut.

The apprentice waited, finding himself unexpectedly anxious to be headed back home. Overhead a few faint stars appeared. Feeling himself disappear into the darkness, he sat still as an owl on a branch, listening.

Hoofbeats sounded a few streets away. A dog barked in the distance. A baby cried out. Suddenly there was an ear-shattering explosion and Lep shot to his feet, dropping the reins.

Another musket, close by, he thought, while Hitabel neighed in terror, reared—and abruptly bolted down the alley.

"Hitabel!" yelled the apprentice. "Whoa!"

Panic-stricken, she raced along, as if trying to strike sparks on the cobblestones. When the alley dead-ended she made a turn to the left. An approaching coach veered sharply to avoid her. A family of mourners scattered like ninepins. With the reins skimming along over the ground, Lep could do nothing but hold tight and shout while she galloped ahead, caught sight of a bonfire, and swerved in terror to her right down a side street.

"Hitabel! Halt, you fool horse!"

On she sped, a torrent of fright, turning when the street butted into a building. Block after block she streaked along. Then gradually she began to grow winded, trotting heavy legged past a dark-windowed church. At last, exhausted, she slowed to a walk, then stopped altogether in the center of the street.

Lep sprang to the ground and snatched up the reins.

Sternly, he stared into Hitabel's face, cursing her fool-headed skittishness, and his own negligence in losing the reins.

"Do you realize what you've done?" he addressed her, and climbed back up in the gig, disgusted that no means existed to make her understand. Winding the reins around his knuckles, he glanced about, wondering where he was—and realized that he wasn't sure exactly where the druggist's shop stood. He hadn't caught the name of the street, nor did he even know the man's name. Dr. Peale hadn't happened to mention it, and the darkness had hidden the name on the sign.

Lep sighed. Then he raised his head and gave the reins a confident shake. If they'd made their way here, they could find their way back—before Dr. Peale even found out they'd gone.

They turned around in the street. It was night now. Lep drove on a ways, then stopped at a corner. In the blackness the brick buildings all looked alike, but he tugged surely on the left-hand rein. Several blocks later he turned to the right, hoping Dr. Peale hadn't discovered what had happened and set out after them himself.

They skipped along briskly and passed a branched streetlamp. Lep halted. It was the first he'd ever seen in his life—and suddenly, staring up at the light, he felt certain he would have remembered if they'd passed the lamp before. Perhaps they'd gone too far, he thought, and struck out down the street to his left.

They clattered on for most of a mile, then stopped at an intersection. A burial cart crossed before them, windows slamming at the coffin's approach. Continuing, Lep became aware that the street had begun to slope downward. He couldn't recall any hills before, yet soon the road was descending steeply. He cocked his ears to a chorus of creaking. He sniffed the air— and at once he knew. He'd somehow reached the waterfront.

The night air was balmy, yet Lep felt chilled. He considered spending the evening roaming the town, shouting Dr. Peale's name, but refused to admit he was that desperate. Glimpsing a coach, he took off after it, intending to ask the way to a druggist, hoping it might be the one he wanted—and halted, realizing that there would be dozens in such a city.

He turned to the right and nosed down an alley. All of a sudden the wheels sounded different. The paving had stopped and Lep tugged on the reins, sensing he'd wandered far off course—and was straying farther every moment.

He looked about, fingers moist with fear. Then feverishly he reached in his pocket and pulled out the paper with Mr. Botkin's address.

"But of course!" he cried out. Hitabel raised her ears. He could spend the night there, while Dr. Peale, no doubt, would beg a bed from the druggist. When daylight came, he'd set off with Clara, find Dr. Peale with

Mr. Botkin's help—and take leave of this confounded town at a gallop.

He shook the reins, sought out a streetlamp, and opened the slip of paper to the light. "No. 8, Elbow Lane" it read, an address he clung to as if for dear life. Searching for someone to give him directions, he noticed a woman walking his way, cleared his throat, and prepared to address her—when suddenly she looked up in horror, then clapped a smelling bottle of vinegar up to her nose and disappeared down an alley.

Block after block he drove on, sending pedestrians scurrying as if he were Death himself. Spotting a lamplighter tramping along, the apprentice drew near.

"Please sir, can you point me to Elbow Lane?"

The man brandished his ladder in defense. "Six blocks up, then turn to your right. And don't come so much as another foot closer!"

"No sir, of course not! And thank you, sir!"

Lep hurried Hitabel up the street, anxious to set eyes on Clara and picturing her surprise. In the morning, he mused, with Mr. Botkin's familiarity with the city, they'd no doubt find Dr. Peale quick as bloodhounds.

Breezing along, Lep reached the sixth corner and made out a sign reading "Elbow Lane." He turned right and headed down the street. Then he stopped.

He jumped to the ground and attached Hitabel securely to a hitching post. Then he dashed down a walk toward a long building, at one end of which he spied No. 8. He charged up the steps two at a time and rapped on the door. He cleared his throat and glanced about. Impatiently, Lep knocked again.

He listened, waiting for the sound of footsteps. Perhaps, he reasoned, Mr. Botkin's work took them away from their rooms in the evenings. He scanned the windows that flanked the door and failed to find any trace of light. Darting around to the side of the building, he spotted a window without a curtain, upon which the light from a streetlamp shone. Hoping he wouldn't be taken for a thief, he grabbed hold of the ledge above his head, hoisted himself up to eye level—and stared inside in disbelief.

Mr. Botkin's quarters were absolutely empty.

Chapter Four

THE THUNDERSTORM SEEKER

Lep heard a whining in his ear and awoke. He rose up from the seat of the gig. It was morning. In bafflement he looked about, then recalled his predicament—and closed his eyes. Praying that the scene about him belonged to the realm of dreams, he all of a sudden slapped at his ear, inspected his palm, and beheld a mosquito. He was awake now, and no denying it. He looked up, found the setting unchanged, eyed the mosquito accusingly, and flicked that cause of his troubles off his hand and into the street.

"Well, Hitabel?" He stepped to the ground and stroked her nose. "Now what do we do?"

He looked into her eyes, but found no answer there. Turning, he studied Mr. Botkin's door and set off down the walk. He rapped with the knocker, sharply, and waited. Then he made a circle of the entire building, stopped again at the uncurtained window, and hauled himself up for another look.

"You, boy!"

Lep froze.

"What's your business? Speak out!"

The voice was behind him. Lep dropped to the ground, whirled around toward the building next door, and found a vulture-nosed man in a nightgown glaring down at him from a nearby window.

"My sister!" sputtered Lep. "She's supposed to be here."

He noticed the window had been raised an inch. The man bent over and put his lips to the crack.

"Don't try your dog tricks on me, you young scamp! There's *nobody* there—as you know full well."

Lep cleared his throat. "But Mr. Botkin—"

"Moved out, with all his belongings," the man hissed. "You'll find nothing there you can steal—now begone!"

The apprentice felt numbed by this news. "But my sister—"

The man slammed the window shut and latched it, waved Lep away, and drew a heavy curtain.

Feverishly, Lep sped around to his door, but the man refused to answer his rapping. The apprentice made desperate use of the knockers on several other doors nearby, without success, and returned to the gig.

"Moved out," he informed Hitabel. But where? Dazed, Lep stared ahead at nothing. There was no telling where they might be found—if they weren't already dead and buried. And at once he recalled that the man had made no mention of a girl with Mr. Botkin.

Lep labored to shoo the thought away.

"Don't you worry, Hitabel," he assured the horse, struggling to take his own advice. He glimpsed the one loaf of bread that remained, and though he knew his stomach must be empty, he felt no desire at all to eat. Hitabel, however, must be hungry, he knew, and he guided her down the street in hopes of finding a common where she could graze.

"Why, we're nearly ready to head home right now," he addressed her, neglecting to mention that he hadn't a notion of where to find Clara, or Dr. Peale, much less the way out of the city.

They clattered through the nearly empty streets, the brick buildings rosy in the morning light. A woman emerged from a grocer's shop and scurried down the sidewalk as quick as a shadow. Keeping his eyes skinned for druggists' shops, Lep discovered they were passing the marketplace—deserted, silent but for the sound of buzzing, the only customers the clouds of flies feasting on the butchers' leavings.

On they plodded, stopping at a corner. Lep noticed a sign reading "Mulberry Street." Spotting a trough of water to his left, he drove up alongside it, let Hitabel drink—and suddenly spun his head around.

Mulberry Street! The name echoed in memory. Puzzled, the apprentice peered at the sign—then his face lit up. Mr. Tweakfield, of course! How could he have been so leather-headed as not to have remembered him sooner? After all, he'd offered his hospitality, in exchange for Lep's tending to Marcus, his footman. He'd said he hoped to find Lep on his doorstep. And he'd even specifically mentioned that he lived at the corner of Mulberry and—

Panic-stricken, Lep ransacked his memory. Mulberry—and Sixth streets, he thought he recalled. Looking up, he saw he was at Mulberry and Second—and, waiting impatiently for Hitabel to stop drinking, he at last snapped the reins and hurried the horse ahead till they came to Sixth Street.

Lep stopped, unsure of which door to try—and wondering whether he'd recalled the right corner. He glanced about. The houses were stately, and just then it occurred to him that Mr. Tweakfield might have left the city. The wealthy had been the first to flee, he remembered hearing—then something caught his eye.

It was a man, in black livery, standing in a doorway, flinging a coat and a pair of breeches onto a heap of clothes outside. He was stocky, with a face as red as raw meat. He stepped back inside and shut the door. The apprentice's eyebrows shot up. It was Marcus.

Overjoyed, he quickly tied up Hitabel, strode down the walk, and knocked on the door. He tucked in his shirt and surveyed the house. It was brick, with white shutters, solid-seeming as a fortress. He raised the brass knocker and pecked again at the door. And suddenly he began to wonder whether Mr. Tweakfield might have forgotten their meeting.

Footsteps approached. Marcus opened the door. Lep recognized his twisted upper lip and recalled his surly, ill-mannered disposition.

"I wonder," Lep stammered, "if you'd tell Mr. Tweakfield that the doctor's apprentice—from Danfield—is here." He swallowed. "Who helped him in August," Lep added. "That is, helped you, sir—with the cut on your head." He paused. "I'm sure he must remember."

Slowly, Marcus unfurled a warm smile.

"Why, of course," purred the footman. "He speaks of you often. Young—Lep, is it not?"

"Yes, sir," said the apprentice, astounded at the man's changed manner.

"Do come in." Marcus stepped aside. "And please allow me to once again offer my thanks for your aid on that day."

Lep couldn't recall Marcus thanking him earlier and gaped at him in wonderment. The footman appeared to have been transformed—his bearing now mild, his voice smooth as cream.

"I'm certain that Mr. Tweakfield will rejoice to find you in Philadelphia." Marcus led the way down a hall, then stopped and smiled upon the apprentice. "Though we shall *all* be joined together soon enough."

The apprentice nodded uncertainly, wondering what the man was referring to.

Knocking softly, Marcus opened a door. "The young doctor from Danfield is here to see you, sir."

Lep gained a view and found the room lined with books.

"Great blazing comets." From behind a stuffed chair a face with thick storm-cloud eyebrows emerged. "My dear Lep—of course!"

The apprentice stepped forward and Marcus closed the door behind him.

"What a fine surprise." Mr. Tweakfield looked haggard. With quivering hands he closed a book. "Take a chair, lad—and tell me what brings you to town."

Obediently, Lep sat down—and told him.

Mr. Tweakfield listened. Then he raised his large body out of his chair and tugged at the cuffs of his velvet coat.

"Have no fear. We'll turn up your traveling companions and have you headed back home in a trice." He raked a strand of gray hair behind his ear. "In the meantime, you will of course stay here. Marcus will see that your horse is cared for, and Mary will soon be serving breakfast."

"If it's any inconvenience at all—"

"Nonsense. I've no other claims on my time, and

for the last several days . . ." Mr. Tweakfield broke off and clutched the book he'd been reading earlier. "In that time I've done little else but read." He scanned his library. "In search of strength."

Lep noticed the scar on the tip of his chin and felt a sudden swell of concern for the man who'd fought with his father at Stony Point.

Just then the serving of breakfast was announced. Lep sniffed food in the air and felt suddenly famished. Walking behind Mr. Tweakfield, he stopped when he sighted the dining-room table and gazed down upon a promised land of herring, potatoes, hot rolls, and cider.

"Eat heartily, gentlemen," murmured the cook, her voice soft as an undertaker's. She was thin as an icicle, and as pale, with a braid of black hair reaching down her back. "We've far more food in the house than we need—given the nearness of the Day."

Mr. Tweakfield took a seat. "Thank you, Mary."

Perplexed, Lep watched her glide out of the room. Then he sat down and noticed the silver serving dishes, wondering to himself what Dr. Peale would think of such opulence.

Mr. Tweakfield began eating and Lep followed suit. Mary reentered with a bowl of plum jam.

"Pardon my interrupting, sir." Her features were frozen and her voice was hushed, as if she were speaking from a prophetic trance. "But I thought you might be interested to know that Mr. Weems, the watchman, informed me this morning that Reading was struck by an earthquake on Sunday."

Lep saw Mr. Tweakfield flinch.

"Lancaster also. And in Bethlehem, the rumbling of the earth is said to have shaken the fruit from the trees."

Mr. Tweakfield whitened. "I'm—grateful for the news."

Marcus set down a silver coffeepot. "No doubt, sir, you noted the large number of falling stars last night also." He turned toward Lep. "Like a rainfall of diamonds. Each one proclaiming the glorious event."

In bewilderment Lep glanced at his host, hoping for illumination, and found him staring down at his plate.

"As it happens," Mr. Tweakfield replied, "I did indeed notice a few."

"And this morning," added Mary, "while absorbed in prayer, I heard a great squawking coming from Emma—and found this underneath her." She reached a hand into her apron pocket and carefully drew out a turquoise duck egg. "Up till now, as you know, all her eggs have been yellow." Spellbound, she fixed her gaze on the prodigy. "A clear sign, to those with eyes to see it, of the coming of the Day."

"The coming of *what* day?" asked Lep, unable to rein in his curiosity another moment.

Marcus smiled. "Why, Lep, the day foreshadowed

by the fever and the other signs—the last day of time! When Gabriel's trumpet will sound in the heavens, the earth and oceans yield up their dead, and all mankind be called to judgment before the magnificent throne of pearl."

Lep peered at the footman in astonishment, recalling his cursing when they'd first met in Danfield and marveling at his newborn piety.

"There's still time, however," continued Marcus, "to prepare yourself, and avoid being cast headlong into the lake of fire." The footman's face glowed like a stove. "By scouring your soul, confessing your sins, and giving your worldly goods to the poor. The latter, so that the Almighty might see that you believed in the coming of his reign, when He shall feed and clothe the righteous. And that the needy might use these goods to settle any remaining debts—and thus be summoned unblemished to the throne."

Ruminating upon this answer, Lep reached for another roll and noticed that Mr. Tweakfield had hardly eaten.

"Mary and I, sir," continued Marcus, "have collected outside a pile of clothes and other belongings we soon shan't require." He stepped forward and took up his master's plate. "I wondered if I might perhaps have leave this morning to give them away."

Mr. Tweakfield gazed at his silver cup. "Yes—of course," he faltered. "By all means."

Mary glanced at the table, at the chairs, at the massive

cabinet full of dining ware. "If you should chance, sir, to change your mind and decide to ready yourself for the reckoning, we shall be glad to aid in relieving your soul of the heavy burden of your many possessions—by distributing them among the destitute."

Lep studied the servants suspiciously, wondering at their excessive regard for their master's spiritual welfare.

"Thank you, Mary," said Mr. Tweakfield. His owlish eyes were focused blankly upon the wall. Then he looked over at Lep and found him finishing his cider.

"If you've eaten your fill, I thought we might set off for an apothecary's shop nearby—in hopes of finding your Dr. Peale."

Lep dabbed at his mouth and stood up. "Gladly, sir."

Mr. Tweakfield rose, fetched a sleek beaver hat, and led Lep out the door past his servants' possessions.

"Don't you fear walking outdoors?" asked Lep.

A woman approaching them quickly crossed over to the other side of the street.

"Nothing to be afraid of," Mr. Tweakfield replied.

Lep, confident in the power of medicine to conquer all ills, was inclined to agree.

"Or so I've always told myself." Mr. Tweakfield, hands clasped behind his back, studied his silver shoe buckles while he walked. "You see, Lep, at your age I fell into a river—and promised myself to God if He'd save me. I caught hold of a tree branch, pulled myself to the bank, and was no sooner dry than I began to

54

wish that I'd never made that particular promise. Poring over volumes on logic and law, I determined that the contract wasn't binding and chose a life, not in church, but rather in court, serving as a lawyer and eventually judge. However—"

Mr. Tweakfield stopped at a corner and took a pinch of snuff from a silver snuffbox.

"I couldn't help but wonder whether God, if He existed, might not strike me dead—and soon began challenging Him to do so, to prove to myself I had nothing to fear. I labored on the Sabbath, studying science and law. I took to speaking the Lord's name in vain—at first in my thoughts, then later out loud. And I found myself strangely compelled to set off on rambling walks—during thunderstorms. Walks from which I returned unscathed."

They passed, as if in review, a row of coffins propped upright against a wall and offered for sale at five dollars apiece.

"Thus you see, Lep, I walk the fever-ridden streets as a pilgrim journeys to the Holy Land." Mr. Tweakfield breathed deeply. "It bolsters my faith—which of late, I confess, appears to be failing."

"Failing?" Lep noticed that Mr. Tweakfield's hands were trembling behind his back.

"First it was my dear wife, Susannah, carried off two years back by the cholera. The following year poor Edmund, my footman—and then Marcus, who would have been felled as well if it hadn't been for you."

Lep restrained himself from mentioning that Marcus had hardly been close to death. And at once he understood Mr. Tweakfield's excessive gratitude that day, and why he'd mistaken the snapping of his coach's spokes for thunderclaps.

"And now the fever—in the streets of my city." Mr. Tweakfield stopped before a druggist's shop, much smaller than the one from which Hitabel had bolted. "Some days I feel convinced that all these omens have indeed been sent from above—and that my own transgression will not go unpunished."

Mr. Tweakfield tried the shop door and found it locked. He knocked twice, peered through the window, and turned toward Lep.

"Don't despair. We'll find your master soon enough."

Lep caught sight of a bill advertising "Dr. Pott's Anti-Pestilential Pills," potent in curing the yellow fever as well as an arklike listing of other afflictions. Scorning such quackery, he spun contemptuously about and set off alongside Mr. Tweakfield, scanning the streets for Dr. Peale. During the course of four hours of roaming they stopped at five other apothecary shops—finding four of them closed and their owners fled, and the fifth operated by a widow in mourning who knew nothing of a doctor from Danfield.

It was nearly three when they arrived back. Mr. Tweakfield approached the door to his house, noticed that the pile of clothes was gone, and spotted in the distance his matched white horses pulling his cart, upon which sat Marcus.

"I've been thinking, Lep, that perhaps I too ought to give up my wordly goods—in hopes of escaping the lake of fire, if there is one."

Lep straightened in alarm. "But, sir, you've led a praiseworthy life of public service—in the courts of law, and on the battlefield. You've no need to leave yourself a pauper, and besides—"

He gestured toward a passing cart carrying a pair of coffins. "The fever's no omen of the end of time. Why, it's nothing more than a trifling disease—which the doctors will soon have stamped out completely."

Mr. Tweakfield sighed, as if wishing to believe him. "And yet, Lep, the earthquakes, and the other signs—"

They walked inside and found dinner waiting. Sitting down, Lep guiltily glanced at the beef, the broth, the peas, the pudding, the cheese.

"It may be," he spoke up, "that it will take another day or two before we find Dr. Peale." He spied his face in the silver spoon set before him. "And though I've no money to pay for my room and board, I can make myself useful, believe me—"

"Nonsense," Mr. Tweakfield replied. "Though I do have one favor to beg, which, if you insist, you may think of as compensating your keep."

"Anything, sir—anything at all."

After eating, Mr. Tweakfield led Lep to the library.

He picked up the book he'd put down earlier and placed it in the apprentice's hands.

"All night I was up reading. My eyes are weary. I wondered if perhaps you'd be so kind as to continue aloud where I left off." Two chairs faced each other across the cramped room, on which Mr. Tweakfield and Lep sat down. "It's a work that's provided great comfort of late."

Lep looked at the book and found it wasn't a Bible, but rather *Experiments and Observations on Electricity* by Benjamin Franklin. The leather cover was worn, the pages supple, as if they'd been turned many times before. Flipping forward to Mr. Tweakfield's place, Lep cleared his throat and commenced to read.

" 'In September 1752, I erected an iron rod to draw the lightning down into my house,' " he recited, and proceeded to describe various experiments in which lightning, the term heavily underlined by Mr. Tweakfield, was described not as the weapon of God's wrath, but simply as a spark of electricity.

Mr. Tweakfield's eyes closed. His hands lay in his lap. He remained attentive to every word, nodding his assent, muttering in agreement, sometimes mouthing the words from memory.

The light left the sky. Lep read on, interrupted but once by Marcus, who brought tea and cast a glance at the book in Lep's hands. Far from growing tired of the task, the apprentice came to feel as if he were nursing a soldier behind the lines of battle. He found himself leaning forward in his chair, declaiming with all the conviction he commanded, intent on healing the patient before him—and imagining him to be none other than his father, lying wounded at Stony Point.

At last Mr. Tweakfield opened his eyes. He thanked Lep and showed him upstairs to his room, where the apprentice was shortly sleeping soundly.

In the morning, Lep rose and drowsily dressed. He inspected his room, strode over to a window, and spied a girl coming down the walk with a basket on her arm.

It was Clara.

Chapter Five

THE INVINCIBLE ANTIDOTE

Lep was struck stiff as a ship's figurehead. Struggling to comprehend how she'd found him, he sighted her blond braids and pink bonnet, knew for certain it was his sister approaching, then flew down the stairs and flung open the door just as she raised her hand to the knocker.

"Clara!" He gawked at her in amazement, as if viewing some speech-snatching wonder of nature.

Clara's eyes expanded. She neglected to breathe. Her arms went limp and her wicker basket fell to the ground with a noisy jingle.

"Why—Asclepius."

The apprentice started. "And who else?" His head was aswirl with thoughts. And suddenly he realized that Clara had had no idea he'd appear.

Lep's eyes glazed over. Cocooned in confusion, he steadied himself against the door post.

"How is it," fumbled Clara, "that you've come to be—here?"

Lep blinked. "Why, searching after *you*. Mother got to worrying so—"

"Worrying?" Clara broke into a smile. "But I'm absolutely safe, believe me."

The apprentice stared at her, dazed and disoriented. "But what then led *you* here—to this very house?"

"Why, my selling, of course." She picked up her basket. "Yesterday I covered Sassafras Street. Today I'll walk Mulberry, and tomorrow High."

"Your selling?"

She produced a red velvet bag from her basket and loosened the drawstring. "Rings."

The apprentice glanced into the bag, then looked up, uncomprehending, at his sister.

"Not just any rings, mind you," she added. She plucked one out and displayed it on her palm. "This, Lep, is one of Mr. Botkin's remarkable *electrical* rings."

"Electrical?" Lep inspected the ring and found that it appeared to be nothing more than a simple band of copper.

"An invincible antidote," continued Clara, "against the pestilence."

Lep froze, gaping dumbfounded at his sister. "The ring?"

"Not by *itself*, of course." She pulled a blue bag from

61

out of her basket. "The rings in the red bag are positive, while these ones here are all negative. Naturally, a person needs both—one on the left hand and the other on the right."

Glancing down at her brother's hands, she was horrified to find him unprotected and quickly produced a pair in his size. "Without them I should have taken the fever long ago."

Quickly she slipped one onto his finger.

Lep yanked it back off. "But I don't *need* your fool rings!"

"And do you expect me to leave you absolutely naked against the yellow fever?"

Lep regarded the rings and sniffed quackery in the air. "And what *good* will they do?"

"What good?" Clara smiled, patiently bearing Lep's ignorance. "The electrical action of the rings, dear brother, serves to draw out the acid from the blood, consuming it and thus destroying the very cause of the yellow fever."

"The cause?" Never had Lep heard of acid in the blood described as the cause of fever—or electrical rings prescribed as its cure.

"Why, they're an infallible protection," piped up Clara. "I shouldn't dream of being without them." She held out her hands, sporting a ring on each. "And Mr. Botkin has set their price at a mere eight dollars a pair."

Astounded, Lep gazed upon his sister. "And is *this*

then the grand commercial opportunity he spoke to us of?"

"Of course," Clara replied, "he couldn't reveal its nature without frightening Mother—or anyone else still unacquainted with electricity's healing powers. Why, in truth, Lep, it's not a matter of commerce, but an endeavor of mercy, so characteristic of Mr. Botkin's generous nature. Someday, his fever-destroying rings will be recognized as the boon that they are—and the name Uzziah Botkin will be revered as belonging to mankind's greatest benefactor."

Lacking confidence in such an outcome, Lep held out the black ring she'd slipped onto his finger and examined it with a jeweler's care.

"Now those, Lep, are made from Egyptian iron, specially treated by Mr. Botkin."

Suspiciously, Lep scraped away a bit of the ring's gummy surface.

"Very costly, it is," continued Clara, "but the best sort of metal for negative rings."

"But Clara—underneath it looks just like copper."

His sister smiled indulgently. "Naturally it *looks* like copper. Especially to someone like you, someone without sufficient experience of the world to be able to tell the difference."

Lep studied the paint on his fingernail and lifted the ring to his nose. "But smell it—it's nothing but copper dipped in tar!"

Clara snatched the ring and eyed it herself.

"And Mr. Botkin," Lep proclaimed, "is nothing more than a charlatan!"

Clara blanched.

"How dare you speak of him so!"

"And how dare you peddle such mockeries of medicine!" Shocked to think that the man he'd once worshiped should stoop to such an enterprise—assisted by his very own sister—Lep swelled with the righteous contempt he'd learned to feel for such posers from Dr. Peale.

"Why, you might just as well be selling bottles of Turlington's Balsam of Life!" he thundered. "Or some other worthless quack-doctor cure!"

"Quack-doctor cure?" Clara tossed out a laugh. "Your ignorance, Lep, amazes me. If you'd seen with those cow's eyes of yours what *I've* seen, you'd know that Mr. Botkin's rings resulted from the most *modern* scientific researches."

Lep rolled his eyes at the words.

"Indeed, that was the very reason we moved to his sloop, the *Angel of Mercy*."

Lep cocked his head. "You moved—to a boat?"

"That's right—anchored out in the Delaware. Each morning I row the skiff to the wharf, sell my wares, buy our food, and row back again—while Mr. Botkin stays and labors over the rings."

Lep's eyes flashed. "So that no one could find you—and discover the shameful trade he lured you into!"

"On the contrary," snapped Clara, "we moved so

64

that he could better pursue his experiments. And without so much as a thought for himself, he sold all his furniture for a pittance, so as to buy the *Angel* and more of the metals—that many more souls might be spared the fever."

"And what might he need a boat for?" asked Lep.

"Why, to electrify the rings, of course—by hanging them over the side in nets." Clara sighed, weary of Lep's backwardness. "It's a well-known fact that the electric fire exists throughout the waters of the earth. Why, the oceans so glow with it at night that a person might thread a needle by its light."

Lep doubted these claims, having never seen an ocean—and knowing that Clara hadn't either.

"I'm afraid," he spoke up, "you'll have to return to threading needles by candlelight soon enough."

Clara stared questioningly at Lep.

"Mother wants you to leave at once."

The girl gasped for air. "Leave—Philadelphia?"

Triumphantly, Lep regarded his sister, secretly glad to be ending her stay and proud to be putting a stop to her ring selling.

"You must never have gotten her letter," said Lep. "She's been tremble-fingered over you for weeks—and the moment I find Dr. Peale, all three of us are heading back home."

Clara gnawed at her lower lip, thinking at a furious pace. Then she sucked in a breath, straightened her spine, peered down at Lep from her two-inch advantage, and suddenly shouted out, "I will not!"

She wheeled about and stormed off down the walk. In a panic, Lep bolted after her.

"But you've got to come—Mother sent us to get you!"

Clara turned left and steamed down the brick sidewalk. "And *I'm* sending you right back again!"

"But the fever!" Lep bustled along beside her.

Clara stopped in her tracks and thrust out her hands. "You may report that I'm wearing the rings night and day—and am therefore in absolutely no danger." Abruptly, she stalked off again, while the apprentice danced about her like a gnat.

"But Clara—"

"I have no intention of leaving—while so many remain in need of the rings."

She rushed down a walk and knocked at a door, received no answer, and marched on, trailed by Lep.

"I wouldn't think of running off from Mr. Botkin," she snapped, her head high, as if addressing the clouds. "It was promised I'd stay for three months—and I will."

"What you *will* do," cried Lep, "is to stop—right this instant."

"As it is," she went on, ignoring Lep's command, "that's only a speck of the debt we owe that generous gentleman."

Lep hustled ahead and stood in her path. Obliviously, she stepped around him.

"A debt," she continued, "I'm proud to repay."

66

In desperation, Lep grabbed at her arm.

"Especially," hissed Clara, glaring at her brother, "to a man whose mission of mercy, with my help, will rescue thousands from the flames of fever!" She shook herself free and continued on her way, refusing to speak another word to Lep. Defeated, weary of capering alongside her, he stopped, a fact she acknowledged with a smile. Refusing to give up, he decided to lie in wait for her at the wharf the next morning and attempt to talk some sense into her. Turning back toward Mr. Tweakfield's, he vowed she'd never get away with this rebellion, and looked forward to finding Dr. Peale. She wouldn't dare to defy *his* command. Why, she'd have no choice but to jump into the gig—quick as a grasshopper, and with no discussion.

The apprentice made out the sound of an ax and spied a man splitting wood across the street. Stepping inside Mr. Tweakfield's door, he inhaled the smell of ham and hot biscuits and saw that breakfast was being served.

"Lep, my lad," Mr. Tweakfield called out. "Out for a stroll this morning, were you?"

"Yes, sir," he mumbled. "In a manner of speaking."

Gliding across the room like a spirit, Mary set butter and jam on the table. "Pardon me, sir," she addressed Mr. Tweakfield. "I realize that you asked for eggs— but in Emma's pen this morning, I found this." She produced from her apron pocket a radish-red duck egg covered with black specks. "It being so clear a sign

67

of the coming, along with the one she laid yesterday, I felt I oughtn't to crack them open."

Mr. Tweakfield's tufted eyebrows shot up. "Can it be," he faltered, "that the Almighty has actually chosen to speak—through our very own Emma?"

Marcus brought coffee, sadly noting through the window the man splitting wood across the street. "Unfortunately, sir, His prophets are most often ignored by the majority of mankind."

Lep looked curiously up at Marcus.

"Mr. Sykes," he continued, "setting his servant to getting in his wood for the winter, is plainly unaware of the fact that winter will never arrive at all." Good-naturedly, Marcus watched the man work. "No doubt his cook is busy with her cutting knife, slicing up mountains of fruit for preserves—while from the tips of his wife's knitting needles falls a torrent of mittens and mufflers and shawls."

He grinned at Lep, seeking to share his amusement.

"And when Mr. Canby on Sassafras Street left for England," Marcus added, "and asked me to watch over his home till he returned sometime *in the spring*—why it was all I could do to humor his wishes without bursting out into a laugh."

"Indeed," murmured Mary, as if to herself, "the plague of flies and mosquitoes worsens, the drought continues, the fever rages." She stared out before her with unseeing eyes. "Death, the fourth rider of the Apocalypse, roams our streets astride his pale horse.

68

Yet still there are those who've yet to perceive that this will be the last year of time."

Mr. Tweakfield's fork slipped from his fingers and clattered to his plate. Endeavoring to compose himself, he smiled shakily in Lep's direction.

"I thought, sir," said the apprentice, anxious to change the subject, "that I might set off in the gig this afternoon." Then he realized that Clara might head back early, perhaps to warn Mr. Botkin. "This morning, that is," he corrected himself.

"Very well." Mr. Tweakfield dabbed at his lips. "Marcus—see that Lep's horse is hitched up."

The footman departed. When they'd finished with breakfast, Mr. Tweakfield led Lep outside and around to the rear of the house, where the gig was waiting.

"I wish to once again offer you my gratitude, Lep, for your vigil last night."

Lep stroked Hitabel, climbed into the gig, and found his eyes fixed on Mr. Tweakfield's scar. "It was nothing," he stammered. "Nothing at all. To be truthful, I should gladly have stayed all night."

Mr. Tweakfield offered a nervous smile. "I took great strength and sustenance from your reading." He scanned the heavens for signs of storm. "Indeed, I shall be sad to see you leave town."

Lep spotted Emma, fat and bride-white, poking about among the weeds. And at once he wondered what would become of Mr. Tweakfield—and his wealth—were he to head home that day.

69

"Surely, sir," the apprentice spoke up, "you're not still considering giving up all you've got—on account of the duck eggs."

Mr. Tweakfield worriedly studied a cloud. "The eggs, of course, are only part of the matter—"

"But duck eggs," asserted Lep, "as you know, can come in all manner of different colors." Emma lifted her head from the weeds, as if aware she was being spoken of. "She might simply have eaten something different. And as for the mosquitoes and the falling stars—"

"Yes, Lep, I know. And no doubt you're correct." Mr. Tweakfield trained his gaze on the ground. "And yet, last night, after you left, I awoke seized with fear, as if gripped by a hawk—and this morning I gave Marcus a very few things, to distribute among the poor. Just in case."

Lep flinched. "But sir—"

"Nothing valuable, mind you. Some books of law and a few other trifles. Nothing of any use to me now."

The apprentice felt dizzy with dismay at this news, as if his own troops had been thrown into retreat.

"But sir," he protested, then chanced to spy Mary step out with a basket of clothes to be dried. Preferring not to be overheard, Lep swallowed his words and took up the reins. "Perhaps I can continue reading this evening."

Mr. Tweakfield's eyes lit. "Why, yes, Lep—of course." He clasped his fluttering hands together. "Perhaps it might restore—my strength."

Lep nodded. Mr. Tweakfield walked toward the house, the apprentice eyeing him protectively. Then he gave the reins a gentle shake and, guiding Hitabel into the street, saw his Latin book slide off the seat— revealing two silver soup spoons beneath.

Lep halted at once. He snatched up the spoons, inspecting them in bewilderment. They resembled Mr. Tweakfield's silverware—and yet how could they have come to be under his book? Had Mr. Tweakfield chanced to glimpse them, he might even have thought Lep had stolen them—the last thing on earth he should ever do.

He put the spoons in a pocket and continued down the street, puzzling over this mystery and wishing he wouldn't so soon be having to abandon Mr. Tweakfield.

Lep sighted the river. Passing a black man driving a cart with three pinewood coffins, he wondered if the occupants might be wearing Mr. Botkin's rings. He sneered at the notion, wincing to think of the money meant for his apprenticeship fee supporting such quackery instead. Determined to separate his sister from Mr. Botkin, he sharpened his eyes for her in case she were about, looked down an alley—and spotted an apothecary's sign.

He drove up before it. The alley was narrow. To his right stood a wooden-handled pump. Lep sensed the scene was twinned in his memory. Then he spied the door knocker in the shape of a pestle—and rejoiced to realize he'd found the very shop that Dr. Peale had entered.

He leaped to the ground and tied Hitabel, praying no muskets would be fired nearby. Dashing down the walk to the shop, he noticed the windows were veiled with curtains—and suddenly the apprentice felt certain that the shop was locked and the owner fled. Preparing himself for a lifetime spent in searching the city for Dr. Peale, he looked about, sighed mightily, fingered the door latch—and found that it opened.

Chapter Six

CALLED TO ARMS

Lep eased the door open. The shop was dim. He stepped inside cautiously, as if he were violating a tomb.

"Yes, sir! And what might I get for you, sir?"

Lep stiffened, and beheld a flounder-lipped face swimming toward him from out of the depths of the shop.

"Why, actually—" Lep fumbled, suddenly aware of the smell of pitch in the air. "In truth, I'm not looking for medicines."

A man halted before him, bald and bowlegged. Around his thick neck he wore a tarred piece of rope that gave him the look of a criminal just rescued from the gallows.

"What I'm searching for," the apprentice continued, "is Dr. Alexander Peale."

"Ah, yes—from Danfield."

Lep's features brightened. The druggist scuttled toward a shelf in the back, as if the gentlemen in question was to be found in one of his cork-topped bottles.

"Unfortunately," he called out to Lep, "Dr. Peale departed. Yesterday."

Lep froze.

"No doubt you're the apprentice he spoke of." The druggist returned from the rear of the shop, his face, pale as candle wax, seeming to light his way.

"Yes, sir," Lep murmured absently. Numbly, he wondered what to do next.

"Well, then—I expect this is meant for you."

Lep's eyes lit up at the sight of a piece of paper the druggist held out in his hand. He grasped it, turned toward the window for light, and found it was a note from Dr. Peale—informing Lep that he could be found at the home of Mrs. Uffington, an old acquaintance who resided at No. 26, Sassafras Street.

"He left about noon," remarked the druggist. "With a medicine chest bursting with Peruvian bark and other cures for the fever."

Lep tucked the paper into a pocket.

"Not that they'll do much good," the man added.

Suspiciously, Lep glanced at the druggist.

"As you're just setting out on the path of doctoring—allow me to offer a spoonful of advice." He eyed his ceiling-high shelves of syrups and powders and potions, and lowered his voice. "You'll pardon my saying such a thing, being an apothecary myself. But there isn't an herb, or pill, or elixir amongst all those jars—or anywhere else—that can cure a case of the yellow fever."

Lep stared at the man in disbelief.

"All you can do is to keep it away," he whispered, touching the rope around his neck. "By sniffing tar all day long, and—what's more important—keeping out of the sun." The druggist admired the gloom in his shop. "Why, you might just as well cut the wood for your coffin, lad, once you let the sun cast your shadow."

Shocked at the man's lack of faith in medicine, Lep declined to thank him for his precious advice, inquired the way to Sassafras Street, and strode briskly out the door.

"No cure for the fever!" he addressed Hitabel, mocking the apothecary's words. He drove down the alley and onto High Street, emerging fearlessly into the sunlight and glaring with contemptuous unconcern at his shadow on the seat. Forcing the druggist out of his thoughts, he glanced about at the great brick buildings that presided over the vacant streets, marveling afresh that this could be the bustling capital city he'd heard of. Noting High Street's impressive width, he tried to imagine the crowds that once filled it—and for a moment he felt that he'd been transported to some city from ancient history, once proud and populous but now long deserted, its avenues empty as dry riverbeds.

Guiding the gig onto Sassafras Street, he stopped before No. 26. The house was vast and armored with ivy—and only a few blocks away, he realized, from Mr. Tweakfield's. Hurriedly tying up Hitabel, he rushed down the walk and rapped with the knocker.

The apprentice heard footsteps. The door opened a crack, through which Lep beheld a cross section of a black serving boy attired in red satin.

"Excuse me," Lep spoke up, "but I'm apprenticed to a doctor—from Danfield—who gave this—"

Quickly, the servant swung open the door, waved Lep inside, and slammed it behind him—and at once the apprentice winced at the nose-scorching air, heavily laden with a cargo of camphor, brimstone, tobacco, and vinegar.

"Mrs. Uffington won't have the doors standing open." The boy was high voiced and a head shorter than Lep. "Lest the outside air get into the house."

Inhaling, with difficulty, her own choking mixture, Lep wondered how she could possibly prefer it to the fresh variety on the other side of the door.

He cleared his throat. "I'm here," Lep continued, "to meet Dr. Alexander Peale."

The servant smiled pleasantly. "Dr. Peale, sir, is gone."

Agape, Lep fixed his gaze on the boy. "Gone?" Why,

he might just as soon try to get a grip on a minnow as catch hold of that man.

"Yes, sir. For the morning, that is. He said that he'd be returning by noon."

Lep's body relaxed, limp with relief. Eyeing the richly furnished parlor, he spotted a sentrylike grandfather clock and saw that it was eleven thirty. Then he spied on the mantel a pair of pewter bowls heaped with smoldering tobacco and turned to ask about them, when Mrs. Uffington appeared at the top of the stairway.

"Isaac—who's here?" she demanded, viewing Lep. Plump, clothed completely in white, she descended the stairs like a cloud with blue eyes.

"A doctor's apprentice, ma'am," answered the servant.

Mrs. Uffington halted three steps from the bottom, ringlets dancing before each ear. "Dr. Peale's lad, is it?"

"Yes, ma'am," Lep replied.

"Very well. Isaac—has our guest been cleansed?"

"No, ma'am."

"Well, set to it, you idle scamp!"

Lep watched with alarm as the boy urgently reached for a bottle by the door, from which he commenced to sprinkle the apprentice with a liquid his eyes surmised to be water—and which his nose discovered at once to be vinegar.

"As a student of medicine," remarked Mrs. Uffington, "you're no doubt aware of the feverous vapors with which our air is contaminated. And the need to take every precaution against them."

Lep managed a nod while enduring his dousing.

"With no rain, lightning, or wind to purify it, the air has grown foul with its own deadly filth. While the rotting animals, the graveyards, and the marshes contribute their own evil exhalations."

Mrs. Uffington ventured one step lower, inspected Isaac's work, and seemed satisfied.

"Many simple souls," she stated, "less knowledgeable than you and I, still cling to the illusion that the air is empty—unaware of the invisible corpuscles, putrid with disease, that teem within it." She inhaled deeply. "Indeed," she added, "this house is but one of the very few islands of health that remain in all the city."

Drenched with vinegar, nostrils prickling, Lep wished he'd washed up on some other shore.

"Show him into the parlor, Isaac—preferably close to the mantelpiece."

Lep followed the serving boy into the room, stopped by the bowls of burning tobacco, and felt as if he were about to be offered for sacrifice at some curious altar.

"Tobacco smoke," asserted Mrs. Uffington, "is a potent purifying agent—as you know." She entered the room, positioned herself in the corner farthest from Lep, and faced Isaac. "To your work, now! There's water to be fetched from the pump—and fresh brimstone to be burned in all the rooms."

Lep watched the servant scurry through the doorway and rush outside with a bucket in his arms.

"Aren't you afraid," the apprentice piped up, "to send him outdoors—with the air so dangerous?"

"Afraid?" Mrs. Uffington gazed at Lep, amazed. "Can it be that you haven't heard? Why, the fact is universally known—that Negroes *cannot catch* the yellow fever."

In surprise, Lep absorbed this fresh knowledge and recalled that every one of the men he'd seen carting coffins to the graveyards had been black.

"And it's a good thing they can't," Mrs. Uffington snapped. "How else would I get food and water—abandoned such as I am?"

"Abandoned?"

She gestured toward the house as a whole. "Do you think I take up a dozen rooms by myself?" She stared at Lep through the haze of smoke. "My husband and three *devoted* daughters caught sight of me shivering in bed last week, took it to be a sign of the fever, and lit out in the coach quick as hares chased by hounds— taking all the servants with them. All except Isaac, who wouldn't leave—and him, just my luck, the laziest of the lot."

She peered out the window at the pump down the street, wondering what was taking him so long.

"And where did they go—your family?" asked Lep.

"Straight to their waiting graves—at a gallop." Mrs. Uffington smiled, savoring the thought.

"Then they're dead?"

"And why else would I be dressed all in white?"

Lep swallowed. "But mourning clothes—are black."

"And do you suppose I'd *mourn* such unfeeling wretches?" She laughed, loudly, as if hoping the sound might penetrate her family's coffins. "On the contrary, it was a joyous occasion to glance out the window that night and behold them."

The apprentice paled. "You saw them—from the window?"

"Not their actual corpses, of course—but the moths."

Lep studied the woman in wonder. *"Moths?"*

"Why, of course!" Mrs. Uffington scowled impatiently. "Surely you're aware that the souls of the dead enter cocoons—and emerge as moths."

Lep pondered this piece of information—and now doubted more surely the others she'd imparted. "But how could you tell they were your husband and daughters?"

"Why, because there were four—one large and three smaller. Fluttering against my bedroom window. *Pleading* with me to let them back in." Like embers blown upon, Mrs. Uffington's blue eyes suddenly glowed brighter. "Which I won't!"

Just then the front door opened. Two sets of footsteps sounded in the hall before it closed.

The apprentice straightened in attention. Then he strode toward the hallway, collided with Isaac—and beheld Dr. Peale dousing himself.

80

"Asclepius! I spied Hitabel—" Reeking of vinegar, he put his hands on Lep's shoulders, then darted into the parlor.

"Lunch, Dr. Peale," Mrs. Uffington announced, "will be served as soon as my slothful servant—"

"Thank you, but I'm afraid I shan't have the time." He took two bottles from his wrinkled black coat and put them in a medicine chest on the floor. "There's a man, Lep—on Spruce Street—who may yet be saved." He closed up the cedar chest. "If we hurry."

Lep tingled, as if hearing a call to arms. "Yes—of course." Forgetting his quest for Clara, he took up the chest, trailed his stooped, stilt-legged mentor out the front door, and breathed in the balmy air with relief.

"That night," Lep blurted out, "Hitabel took fright, from a musket—while you were in the shop. And by the time she stopped—"

"Yes, I heard the blast." They climbed into the gig, took off, and passed two children smoking cigars for protection. "I'm just thankful you're safe—we can trade tales later. At the moment, however, there's something more pressing." He glanced at Lep. "I've decided to remain in the city—until the fever passes."

Openmouthed, the apprentice eyed Dr. Peale.

"In evicting all trace of vanity from my spirit, I vowed to serve others and must do so now. Especially here, in Philadelphia, the scene of my folly—and now, my atonement."

Dr. Peale hurried Hitabel onward. "The city writhes

in its agony, Lep, abandoned by all but a few of its doctors. After curing Mrs. Uffington of a trifling distemper that sent her household fleeing for their lives, I treated the woman next door for the fever—and was at once surrounded by a swarm of supplicants, piteously begging my aid. And such, I'm afraid, will be the case until cold air arrives—perhaps in a fortnight—and the fever subsides, as is its habit." He turned down a side street, raising a congregation of crows from a stiff-legged dog. "However, I have a duty to your mother, and must insist that you take the gig yourself and transport Clara—"

"But Clara is gone!" Roused by Dr. Peale's oration, Lep made up his mind to stay with his master—and not to depart until the fever was conquered. "That is—she's moved to another address. But she's safe!" Or believed she was, he thought, and *would* be once he convinced her to give up roaming the streets all day selling rings. "And I should like to remain and help as well! I've a place to stay, just a few blocks away—at the home of the man I helped on the road."

Dr. Peale contemplated the matter.

"To be honest, I should fear to send you back by yourselves. Perhaps it would be an even graver lapse of duty than to keep you here."

He turned down an alley and cast his eyes across at his apprentice.

"Very well. I'll write to your mother at once, and report that Clara is not to be worried over. And that your own assistance is desperately needed." He drew to a halt and hopped down. "Which it is."

They crossed the street toward a shabby brick building, entered one of a row of rooms, and prevailed over the powerful stench that greeted them, guardsmanlike, at the door.

"I was brought here to Mr. Greeves last night, by his sister," Dr. Peale announced. He strode up to a mattress leaking straw, on which Lep beheld a shirtless man, withered as a December cornstalk. "As it is, I fear we may be too late."

Grimly, Lep looked down upon the first case of yellow fever he'd ever seen. The man's face was purplish, his eyes pale yellow. Red marks, like mosquito bites, dotted his throat. Lep saw that he'd vomited up some dark matter, opened his watch, took the man's pulse, and found his arm dry as a cast-off snakeskin.

"His heart's scarcely beating," the apprentice reported. The patient stared out with an unseeing gaze, his eyelids rising and falling like shutters blown aimlessly back and forth by a breeze.

"A dose of the bark, given with brandy, may yet turn the tide," Dr. Peale declared. He prepared the potion and struggled to get it down the throat of his stuporous patient. "And yet, Lep, you'll find that once the black vomit comes up, there's often little hope."

Lep glanced around the room, found a cloth, and wiped the foul-smelling trail that led from the patient's mouth.

"The red pustules," added Dr. Peale, "as there on his throat, are likewise a sign—most often, that Death will soon pay his visit." He reached into the medicine chest for a bottle of vinegar and handed it to Lep. "And if you mean to keep him from calling on you, you'd best drench your handkerchief in this and breathe through it when you're attending a patient."

Dutifully, Lep accepted the bottle, though he felt he had little to fear from the fever. After all, he was a doctor, or nearly so—empowered to battle Death himself, elevated above the rank of most mortals and interceding, saintlike, on their behalfs.

"Additionally," Dr. Peale spoke up, "you'd best wear this around your neck." He offered Lep a white pouch filled with camphor. "Since you'll be constantly meeting the fever at close hand."

The apprentice sniffed at the sharp-smelling camphor. "Is Mrs. Uffington right, then—that the air is diseased?"

Dr. Peale shook his head and sighed. "Her father was a doctor, an acquaintance of mine, who feared the fresh air as other men fear poison. She stands by his theories, unaware that the contagion lives not in the atmosphere, but in its victims—and that camphor and vinegar are needed only when coming into close contact with the sick."

He stepped on two bedbugs—creatures closely related to the vile beetles, he was sure—raised a shade, and threw open a window. Noting a flock of drab-

Chapter Seven

THE IMPOSTER

Lep stood and gazed at the name, paralyzed, seeming to belong to the army of tombstones assembled at attention around him.

He reached out and felt the letters, as if blind. "Botkin" was uncommon, he thought to himself, but "Uzziah Botkin"—why, the name had to be rare as a black-feathered swan, or rarer. Studying the stone, he saw that the man had died in 1778. The year, Lep mused, before his own birth, and the same year his father had finished repaying the last of the loan to Mr. Botkin—after which there'd been no news of the man.

Suddenly, Lep knew *why* he'd not been heard from. Mr. Uzziah Botkin had died—and the man who'd carried off Clara was an impostor!

colored birds sunning themselves in the street, Dr. Peale smiled, glad that their shamelessly proud spring plumages were no longer to be seen.

"And is it true," Lep asked, "that Negroes are free of the fever, as Mrs. Uffington believes?"

Dr. Peale squatted over his medicine chest, busily concocting a syrup. "The notion is widespread, but unfounded, I'm afraid. Only yesterday afternoon I lost a Negro woman to the fever—and this morning her husband and their infant child."

Lep thought at once of Isaac, the serving boy.

"I'm afraid Mrs. Uffington is untrustworthy as a teacher," Dr. Peale declared. "And with her family fled, she's nearly unbalanced, so that I feared to leave her in her condition."

Lep, likewise relieved not to have to abandon Mr. Tweakfield, returned his attention to Mr. Greeves. "And what course of treatment do we follow with the fever?"

Dr. Peale administered his syrup. "Warm baths and stimulants in the early stage. Later the Peruvian bark, cold drinks, plus laudanum and spirits as needed." He removed the vinegar-soaked cloth from his mouth. "No food beyond barley water. Fresh air. And attention to keeping the bedding clean."

Committing this list to memory, Lep opened the only other window, sponged Mr. Greeves with cool vinegar, got him to swallow a cup of cold water, and changed his filthy linen. After which, like a Roman soldier's shield bearer, he raised the medicine chest in his arms and followed his master out the door, accompanying him to a series of bedsides—visits for which Dr. Peale staunchly refused to accept the slightest payment. When at dusk they returned to Mr. Greeves, they found his sister present—and the patient dead.

" '*Nihil est omnino beatum,*' " Dr. Peale muttered as they set off in the gig.

Lep nodded. " 'Not everything comes out happily.' "

"Horace, I believe." Dr. Peale turned up Sixth Street. "We'll consider that your Latin lesson for the day."

At the corner of Mulberry, Lep climbed down. Entering Mr. Tweakfield's house, he explained the change in plans and found his host insistent that Lep—and his sister as well—should stay as long as they liked, at the agreed-upon price of Lep's reading in the evenings. A compensation he was pleased to provide that night until finally, at midnight, he trudged up to his room and sank into sleep.

Swiftly, the sun invaded the sky, scattering night and taking possession of the heavens. Hoping to catch Clara at the wharf before he joined Dr. Peale, Lep hurriedly dressed, removed the two silver spoons from his pocket, and set them on his table, intending to inquire about them later.

He charged outside and down the street. Streaking along, he recalled the passage he'd read aloud the night before—giving proofs that the luminescence of the sea

was *not* the result of electricity. He was certain now that Mr. Botkin's fever-fighting worthless, and was left wondering only man as he could have changed so drastical

Cutting across a graveyard, Lep prepared his speech to Clara, thundering against her and proposing she join him in nursing th stopped abruptly, his eye caught by the imposing granite gravestone.

He backed up and stared at the stone, wo The large chiseled letters spelled "Uzziah colored birds sunning themselves in the street, Dr. Peale smiled, glad that their shamelessly proud spring plumages were no longer to be seen.

"And is it true," Lep asked, "that Negroes are free of the fever, as Mrs. Uffington believes?"

Dr. Peale squatted over his medicine chest, busily concocting a syrup. "The notion is widespread, but unfounded, I'm afraid. Only yesterday afternoon I lost a Negro woman to the fever—and this morning her husband and their infant child."

Lep thought at once of Isaac, the serving boy.

"I'm afraid Mrs. Uffington is untrustworthy as a teacher," Dr. Peale declared. "And with her family fled, she's nearly unbalanced, so that I feared to leave her in her condition."

Lep, likewise relieved not to have to abandon Mr. Tweakfield, returned his attention to Mr. Greeves. "And what course of treatment do we follow with the fever?"

Dr. Peale administered his syrup. "Warm baths and stimulants in the early stage. Later the Peruvian bark, cold drinks, plus laudanum and spirits as needed." He removed the vinegar-soaked cloth from his mouth. "No food beyond barley water. Fresh air. And attention to keeping the bedding clean."

Committing this list to memory, Lep opened the only other window, sponged Mr. Greeves with cool vinegar, got him to swallow a cup of cold water, and changed his filthy linen. After which, like a Roman soldier's shield bearer, he raised the medicine chest in his arms and followed his master out the door, accompanying him to a series of bedsides—visits for which Dr. Peale staunchly refused to accept the slightest payment. When at dusk they returned to Mr. Greeves, they found his sister present—and the patient dead.

"*'Nihil est omnino beatum,'*" Dr. Peale muttered as they set off in the gig.

Lep nodded. "'Not everything comes out happily.'"

"Horace, I believe." Dr. Peale turned up Sixth Street. "We'll consider that your Latin lesson for the day."

At the corner of Mulberry, Lep climbed down. Entering Mr. Tweakfield's house, he explained the change in plans and found his host insistent that Lep—and his sister as well—should stay as long as they liked, at the agreed-upon price of Lep's reading in the evenings. A compensation he was pleased to provide that night until finally, at midnight, he trudged up to his room and sank into sleep.

Swiftly, the sun invaded the sky, scattering night and taking possession of the heavens. Hoping to catch Clara at the wharf before he joined Dr. Peale, Lep hurriedly dressed, removed the two silver spoons from his pocket, and set them on his table, intending to inquire about them later.

He charged outside and down the street. Streaking along, he recalled the passage he'd read aloud the night before—giving proofs that the luminescence of the sea was *not* the result of electricity. He was absolutely certain now that Mr. Botkin's fever-fighting rings were worthless, and was left wondering only how such a man as he could have changed so drastically.

Cutting across a graveyard, Lep prepared in his mind his speech to Clara, thundering against her ring selling and proposing she join him in nursing the ill—then stopped abruptly, his eye caught by the name on an imposing granite gravestone.

He backed up and stared at the stone, wonderstruck. The large chiseled letters spelled "Uzziah Botkin."

Chapter Seven

THE IMPOSTER

Lep stood and gazed at the name, paralyzed, seeming to belong to the army of tombstones assembled at attention around him.

He reached out and felt the letters, as if blind. "Botkin" was uncommon, he thought to himself, but "Uzziah Botkin"—why, the name had to be rare as a black-feathered swan, or rarer. Studying the stone, he saw that the man had died in 1778. The year, Lep mused, before his own birth, and the same year his father had finished repaying the last of the loan to Mr. Botkin—after which there'd been no news of the man.

Suddenly, Lep knew *why* he'd not been heard from. Mr. Uzziah Botkin had died—and the man who'd carried off Clara was an impostor!

But who? The apprentice looked to his left and spied the grave of Mr. Botkin's wife, Judith. Knowing that name to be correct, he was certain now who lay buried at his feet. Scurrying to his right, he found other Botkins—Jeremiah, Joseph, Augustus. Then he halted, all of a sudden recollecting part of the deceiver's tale—that his brother Ulysses had been buried in the family plot the previous winter. Surely, he reasoned, the man would never have risked being spotted for a fraud by Lep's mother by making mention of a brother of Mr. Botkin's who'd never lived. Yet, darting about the graves like a bat, Lep failed to find a headstone for Ulysses—then stopped, realizing the reason. Ulysses Botkin was still alive—and had cloaked himself in his dead brother's name!

Quickly Lep looked around, fixed the location of Mr. Botkin's grave, then lit out toward the wharf at top speed. No wonder, he thought, the Mr. Botkin who'd shown up in Danfield had been dressed in tatters—for this was the brother who'd failed in his ventures, and was now reduced to quackery for a living. No doubt he'd heard of the Nyes from his brother, and had counted on the news of Uzziah's death never reaching a mere crossroads like Danfield. Lep ground his teeth at the thought of the scoundrel. Full of twists as a pig's tail, he was.

He sped down the center of High Street, bursting with impatience to tell Clara what he'd found. She'd have *no choice* but to shed the villainous Mr. Botkin—and his good-for-nothing rings—once she learned the truth.

Fearing he might miss her if he wasn't quick, he waved to a man who was cleansing a newspaper by holding it with tongs above a smoking tar barrel.

"Can you tell me, sir, which way to the wharf?"

The man stared across the street at Lep in wonder. "The *wharf?*"

Lep halted. "The *wharf!*" he repeated, annoyed at losing even a moment.

The man puzzled over Lep's question and cast a glance into the tar barrel, as if consulting an oracle.

"Begging your pardon," he spoke up at last. "But *which* wharf is it you're looking for?"

Lep stiffened. "You mean to say there's more than one?" Having never been to a city before, he'd had no idea of what to expect.

"Aye, lad—more than one." The man waved the newspaper about in the smoke. "In truth, there be close to ninety of 'em."

"*Ninety?*"

Lep swallowed, dismayed. Then he rushed down the street.

He only recalled Clara mentioning "the wharf"—she'd never specified which one. Reaching the riverfront, he looked about. His sister was nowhere to be seen. Dashing out to the end of the wharf before him, he found no sign of the skiff she said she used, nor of Mr. Botkin's *Angel of Mercy.*

He scurried to the ends of the neighboring wharves without finding any trace of Clara. Then something else she'd said sprang to mind—that she'd be doing her selling on High Street that day. Rushing back the way he'd come, Lep turned up the street and searched block after block, finally stopping to rest against a pump.

He glanced about. Where in blazes could she be? He wondered if she might be at some sufferer's bedside, a few yards away but hidden from view, slipping the rings onto trembling fingers. Or perhaps she'd switched streets to keep him and Dr. Peale from finding her—merrily unaware that she was loyally serving an impostor.

The thought filled the apprentice with rage. Pulling out his watch, he opened it up and was amazed to find it was after nine. Dr. Peale must be waiting for him—if he hadn't left on his rounds already. He'd have to hunt up that confounded sister of his another time.

Closing the watch, he hurried to Mrs. Uffington's, and was relieved to be let in by his master himself.

"I'm sorry—to have kept you from our patients," said Lep.

Dr. Peale shut the door. "As it happens, you haven't."

Lep glimpsed Mrs. Uffington in the parlor and quickly sprinkled himself with vinegar.

"Unhappily, our work begins here this morning."
Dr. Peale pursed his lips. "Young Isaac, I'm afraid."

Lep froze. Dr. Peale set off down the hall.

"The—yellow fever?" Lep stuttered.

"Without doubt."

Lep bolted forward.

"Without doubt, indeed!" Mrs. Uffington, attired in blinding white like an earthly comet, blazed out of the parlor, trailing them down the smoke-filled hall to a tiny room in the rear of the house. Inside, shivering in his bed, lay Isaac.

"I'm afraid," said Dr. Peale, "that the early symptoms are all clearly present." He looked into the patient's fearful eyes. "Chills. Weak pulse. A state of languor. Tongue pale, and complaints of pains in the back."

"But the boy is black!" Mrs. Uffington cried. "He can no more catch the yellow fever than sprout wings and commence to fly with the birds!"

Quivering like a poplar leaf, Isaac mutely stared up at his mistress.

"It's perfectly plain to me," she continued, "that the scamp is *pretending* a case of the rattles, in hopes of a holiday from his chores. And that the only sickness he suffers from is a case of pernicious idleness, an ill that infects *all* the servant class—the only cure for which is work!"

Dr. Peale sighed, faced Mrs. Uffington, and winced at what he regarded as an excessive display of fine lace.

"May I remind you that I'm a trained physician, educated in Edinburgh—" Suddenly Dr. Peale broke off, mortified at the thought that he might seem to be boasting of being trained abroad. Praying for humility, he lowered his eyes, and was restored by the pleasing sight of a pair of holes in his stockings.

"The boy," he began again, "is ill. I've already given him a hot bath and some wine and covered him up with such blankets as I could find. He must be kept warm and supplied with hot drinks. Molasses and water, heated, will do fine."

Abashed, Mrs. Uffington glared at the doctor. "A fine state of affairs! My serving boy rests—while *I* run about and wait on *him*!"

"In the course of our travels," Dr. Peale replied calmly, "Lep and I will be more than happy to purchase whatever food you require."

Mrs. Uffington scowled. "And who's there to cook it?"

"We'll be glad to give you what help we can." Dr. Peale turned and struck out down the hall. "At the moment, however, we've more patients to attend to."

Quickly, Lep fetched two buckets and filled them with water from the pump down the street. Setting them down in Mrs. Uffington's kitchen, he was instructed to purchase a long list of items, beginning with nutmegs and ending with brimstone, after which he took up the medicine chest and followed his master out the front door.

"Infallible preservatives against the plague!" cried a woman, strolling down the street with a basket full of bottles.

Dr. Peale frowned. "I believe," he said, "you're now familiar with the *proper* course of treatment for the fever."

Lep stared at him quizzically. "Yes, sir. I believe so, sir."

They climbed into the gig. Dr. Peale shook the reins. "As the ill are so numerous and the doctors so few, I believe it best that we work alone, in hopes of reaching more of the stricken."

A gust of excitement swept over Lep.

"We'll get you a chest of supplies at my druggist's and begin our work in Appletree Alley. Where, it grieves me greatly to say, I'm sure we can find enough patients for both of us."

"Yes, sir!" The apprentice beamed at his master. "Appletree Alley! Splendid, sir!"

Ravenously hungry, reeking of vinegar, Lep entered Mr. Tweakfield's house at dusk, set down his own cedar medicine chest, and found his host seated in the library, contemplating an egg at arm's length.

"One of Emma's?" inquired the apprentice.

Absently, Mr. Tweakfield nodded. The shell was green and covered with black squiggles.

"Never has she produced such an egg before." Gloomily, he gazed upon it, as if its markings spelled out his own doom. "It's not easy," he murmured, "to dismiss such a sign. Indeed, I sometimes entertain the notion that the drought, the earthquakes, and even the fever itself have all been called forth on my account— a grand demonstration of the Almighty's presence. And a proof that my broken promise was recorded and still remains to be paid for—with the wealth I acquired through my secular calling."

Alarmed at Mr. Tweakfield's dangerous state, Lep turned toward the bookshelf, as to his medicine chest, and reached for Priestley's *History and Present State of Electricity*. Ignoring his hunger, he commenced to read of attractive and repulsive forces, the nature of the electrical fire—and the causes of thunderstorms, among which no mention of divine punishment was made.

Stopping his ministrations only to devour the dinner brought him by Marcus, the apprentice recited far into the night. At last Mr. Tweakfield, restored by the treatment, lifted his large body from his chair, thanked Lep, and led the way up the stairs.

"By the way," he remarked, stopping midway up. "While changing the linen on your bed this morning, Mary came on two soup spoons—tucked under the mattress."

Lep halted, stunned. "Under the mattress?" He distinctly recalled laying them on the table.

"I believe that she reported finding a silver tray as well."

"A *tray?*" Lep peered into Mr. Tweakfield's eyes.

"But I never brought any such thing to the room! And as for the spoons—"

Mr. Tweakfield eyed his guest. "I don't for a moment doubt your honesty, Lep, and never meant to imply you were stealing. I've no notion what the articles were doing there—and as they've been found, I don't much care."

He moved up the stairway, followed by Lep. Entering his room, the apprentice at once reached his hand under his mattress for whatever else might be there. Finding nothing, he blew out his lamp, sure that the silver pieces hadn't crawled under his mattress on their own. On the contrary, he felt certain they'd been deliberately placed, in hopes of turning his host against him, by the only hands that could possibly have done it—those of Mr. Tweakfield's servants.

At daybreak Lep was at the waterfront, combing the wharves near Mulberry Street. He seethed to think of Clara selling Mr. Botkin's rings, devotedly preying on the ill and fearful on behalf of a man who'd swapped names, told lies, and tricked Lep's mother into a loan—a loan, Lep suddenly realized, the scoundrel most likely didn't mean to repay. He cursed Clara's ignorance of the man—and the fact that he couldn't enlighten her. Somehow, he had to find her.

Two hours later, having searched in vain, he headed for Mrs. Uffington's. He sprinkled himself with vinegar upon entering and found Dr. Peale by Isaac's bed, staring down at the patient's sweat-filled face.

"Dissatisfied with my first course of treatment, I've bled the boy in hopes of greater success."

Lep pricked up his ears at the news of this change. Mrs. Uffington, grasping a white shawl around her shoulders, marched in and aimed a knowing scowl at Isaac. "In addition," continued Dr. Peale, "I've decided to abandon the use of warm baths." He turned toward Mrs. Uffington. "I wish you to seat him in a tub each two hours and throw a bucket of *cold* water upon him— that the morbid heat might be carried away."

"And his scheming slothfulness as well!" Mrs. Uffington, her face pale as her clothing, wrapped her shawl more tightly around her. "A slave in my own house, I am—while my servant sleeps the day away!"

Dr. Peale made no answer, lowered his shoe on a bedbug, and walked out of the room. Relishing the notion of Mrs. Uffington laboring on behalf of Isaac, Lep followed behind his mentor, and the two left to make their rounds.

At five o'clock the pair returned. Lep noticed Mrs. Uffington leaning back in a chair in the corner of the parlor—and was immediately struck by the suspicion that she'd reclined there all day, refusing to attend Isaac.

Outraged at the thought and determined to find out, he gathered his courage, stalked into the parlor, strode up to Mrs. Uffington—and was deflated at once by the sound of her madly chattering teeth.

97

His intended words fled. He stared at the woman. She was clutching her shawl, her face pallid as ice.

Lep called his master. Dr. Peale hurried in, viewed her tongue, sampled her pulse, inspected her eyes and the red spots on her arms, and, declaring that she had the yellow fever, rushed her upstairs to her room.

Chapter Eight

THE TRAITOR

All night Mrs. Uffington writhed with the fever, while Dr. Peale worked mightily to expel it. He began with brandy, modest bloodletting, and buckets of cold water thrown over her hourly. As she showed no improvement, he tried bark and opium, applied poultices to her throat and arms, and, looking with greater hope to his lancet, increased his bleedings to thirty-five ounces.

That night there was a frost, the second of the season. During the next four days the number of new cases of fever steadily declined and those who'd fled the city began returning. Lep found the streets suddenly filled with people as he searched, each morning, for the sight of Clara among them. He wondered if he'd ever chance to find her, or whether Mr. Botkin, hearing from her that Lep and Dr. Peale were in the city, had hauled up his anchor and carried her off.

Upon arriving at Mrs. Uffington's each day, Lep administered Isaac's remedies. Mrs. Uffington, however, would not be touched by Lep and, despite his master's crowd of patients, insisted that Dr. Peale alone should administer his constantly revised regimen: mercurial purges, preparations of camphor, ointments intended to stimulate the liver, a diet of toast, supplanted by tea, replaced by ripe fruit and mutton broth.

At noon on the fifth day of her sickness, with a score of beds yet to visit, many of whose occupants were in a critical stage, Dr. Peale dispatched Lep back to the house with instructions to give Mrs. Uffington her treatment—despite all protestations.

Lep found her in no condition to object. She was dewed with sweat and gasping for breath, wrapped in a delirium. Her pulse was furious, her skin yellow and hot. Blood was flowing from her nose and gums. She called out words, yet was unaware of his presence. Grateful for this fact, Lep opened his chest and, meticulously duplicating Dr. Peale's treatment, mixed an elixir of Peruvian bark, faithfully following his master's proportions.

Mrs. Uffington sat up. "Moths!" she cried out.

She stared wide-eyed before her but seemed not to see Lep, who, hoping he might escape undetected, quickly cajoled his concoction down her throat.

"Not four, as there've always been—but five!"

Lep clapped a vinegar-soaked cloth to his mouth and administered an opuim pill. Working rapidly, he mixed up a mustard plaster and applied it to her forearms and throat, in hopes of drawing out the fever. Then he reached for his lancet and his graduated bowl and, shadowing his master exactly, made three short cuts in her upper arm.

Abruptly, Mrs. Uffington's eyelids lifted.

"Five moths!" she burst out. "Three small—and two large!"

Lep glanced at the window beside her bed but failed to see any moths.

"My soul has departed—and joined my family!"

Lep studied his bowl. Then he looked up at his patient—and was startled by her changed expression.

"What are you doing here?" she whispered.

Lep swallowed, saw he'd drawn thirty-five ounces, and speedily bandaged her arm.

"Dr. Peale couldn't come—so he sent me instead. And I followed his treatment to the letter—believe me. No doubt you'll throw off the fever quite soon."

Struggling for breath, ignoring his trespassing, Mrs. Uffington peered up into Lep's large brown eyes. "Do you really believe so?"

"But of course!" he replied, rushing to defend the powers of medicine. "The bark by itself has cured many cases! And blisters and bleeding are well known to be potent in draining the morbid heat from the body."

He mopped her brow with a cloth dipped in vinegar, packed up his chest, and strode confidently out the door.

Throughout the remainder of the afternoon Lep found Mrs. Uffington inhabiting his thoughts, fearing he might have neglected some tiny detail of Dr. Peale's instructions—the consequences of which would be his to bear. Returning in the late afternoon, he darted upstairs and looked into her room, shaky with dread.

She lay still under the sheets. Her eyes were half open.

"Lep?"

The apprentice approached her bed.

"I believe," she said softly, "the fever's departing."

Lep's body slackened with relief.

"Just as you said it would earlier."

Lep found her pulse slower. "I'm happy to hear it." Having satisfied himself that he hadn't killed her after all, he turned to go.

"And Lep," she continued.

He turned around.

"I'll not have Dr. Peale laying his hands on me any longer."

Lep stared down at the woman, dismayed. "But I gave you the identical treatment that he himself has administered the past three days."

Mrs. Uffington managed a flickering smile. "But it's you who've succeeded in driving out the fever. And

I'll have no other doctor on earth attending me."

She gazed gratefully up at Lep. The apprentice smiled back uncertainly. Then he reported her wishes to Dr. Peale and set out toward Mr. Tweakfield's.

He passed a woman whose yellow skin showed her to be a survivor of the fever. Lep thought of Mrs. Uffington's improvement, wondering whether the credit could actually belong to him, as she claimed. He glowed with a sudden sensation of pride—then quickly cast the thought out of his head. He was relieved that Dr. Peale had not seemed affronted by Mrs. Uffington's choice and, reminding himself that he was but an apprentice, vowed to follow his master's instructions with unquestioning devotion and a humble spirit.

He turned a corner—and came to a halt. A block ahead he sighted a girl carrying a basket—Clara!

Instantly, Lep bolted toward her, desperate to pry her from Mr. Botkin—then just as quickly he came to a stop, realizing his search wasn't over. The girl he'd spied turned out to be an old woman, carrying not a basket of rings but rather a plucked chicken by the neck.

Early the next morning Lep set off for the river. Having investigated Powell's Wharf, Ball's Wharf, Warner's, Meredith's, and a dozen others, he decided to try those near Chestnut Street, struck out down Pemberton's Wharf—and nearly bowled over Clara.

103

"Why—Lep. I'd expected you'd left by now."

The apprentice stared at her in amazement, hardly able to believe his eyes.

"Or have you come to your senses and decided to purchase a pair of the fever-devouring rings?"

Lep shook his head, spied her skiff, and viewing the vast river before him, faintly sighted through the morning mist a single-masted ship with the words *Angel of Mercy* on its stern.

"I've got something to show you." He grabbed her wrist. "Something that might bring *you* to your senses."

He turned and hauled her toward the graveyard.

"Lep—I demand you release me this instant!" Her basket of rings jingled shrilly. "I've got work to attend to—and no time for your pranks."

The apprentice tightened his grip and marched on.

"And I've told you my mind is made up to remain and aid Mr. Botkin in his life-saving endeavor—the merest *fraction* of the debt we owe him."

"On the contrary," snarled Lep, "we owe him *nothing!*"

Clara whitened, as if he'd blasphemed in church.

"How dare you speak so! And with regard to a man whose generosity shines like a beacon."

Briskly, Lep led her into the graveyard.

"A man who deserves our eternal thanks—and for whom I should gladly labor for life!"

Lep halted abruptly and, as if in reply, reached out

his hand toward Mr. Botkin's tombstone.

Clara's eyes widened. Lep let go her arm—then grabbed it again to keep her from falling.

"*There,*" he declared, "is the man to whom we owe our eternal gratitude."

Desperately Clara glanced about, as though hoping to find the grass merely painted, the headstones paper, and the whole scene a sham.

"The man you're aiding is *Ulysses* Botkin—whose wondrous generosity has consisted of posing as his brother, deceiving us out of two candlesticks, and acquiring three months of your labor at no charge."

Clara touched the grainy granite. "Perhaps," she stammered hopefully, "there happened to be another Uzziah Botkin."

"*In Philadelphia?*" Lep pounced upon her. "Buried beside a wife named Judith? And just happening to die in the very year that all news of Mr. Botkin ceased?"

Clara stared vengefully at the gravestone, chagrined at being shown up by her brother.

"But the rings—" she spoke up, her eyes suddenly bright. "They're still potent, even if the man *is* a poser."

"Potent?" Lep snorted contemptuously. "It so happens that just the other day I was reading a book by Benjamin Franklin himself—in which he explains why the light in the oceans can't possibly come from electricity, as Mr. Botkin told you. And besides, he doesn't soak his rings in the sea—but in the Delaware river!"

"Which he says," shot back Clara, "contains properties that render it far superior to the sea."

"And he *also* said he was Uzziah Botkin!"

Uncertainly, Clara eyed the rings on her fingers.

"He didn't move to the boat for the sake of science at all," Lep insisted, "but most likely to make sure Mother wouldn't find out his work. And so that once he's squeezed the last shilling from the fever he can raise his anchor and get away in a hurry, before he's tarred and feathered for his villainy—and no doubt without repaying our loan."

Glumly, Clara wondered if Lep was right. "But he's already sold the candlesticks."

"How much did he get?"

"Fifty dollars, I think."

"Very well. That's how much you'll take in return."

Clara's eyelids jerked up. "Take?"

Lep sighed. "It's *our* money—and set aside for Dr. Peale. I'm not about to give Mr. Botkin the chance to scamper free with it."

Clara stared at her brother. "But how?"

"Tonight, while he's sleeping, take fifty dollars and put it in the trunk you brought, along with all of your other things. Then hop into the skiff and row to the wharf."

Clara swallowed. "But the trunk's heavy—and the skiff's four feet down from the deck of the boat. It took both of us to get it on the boat when we came."

Lep studied the ground, deep in thought.

"Tonight, then, just hide the trunk on the deck. In the morning, row into the wharf as usual, pick me up, and row back again. You'll tell Mr. Botkin you forgot something or other, make certain he's settled securely in the cabin, then hand the trunk down to me—and row off."

Anxiously, Clara pondered the plan. "But what if he spots you as we approach the boat?"

"I'll bring along something to hide myself under."

"And what if he wants to come out of the cabin?"

Lep recalled Dr. Peale's druggist. "Just tell him it's been proven that the rays of the sun can bring on the fever—of a sort not even his rings can cure."

"You're sure that'll work?"

Lep looked at his watch and realized Mrs. Uffington was awaiting him. "Just tell him it's *scientific,*" he replied acidly. "But right now I've got to go."

"Tomorrow morning, then," Clara piped up. "At Pemberton's Wharf."

"I'll be waiting," said Lep, and set off down the street.

He headed for Mrs. Uffington's, stepped inside, climbed the stairs, and was startled to find her fully dressed and standing beside the window.

"You're late," she declared.

Lep studied the woman, astounded at her recovery. Her skin remained yellowish, but the sweating and spasms seemed at last to have left her.

"I'm sorry, ma'am." He mixed up a syrup, following

his master's specifications. "But with the way you've improved, it appears you'll be able to care for yourself soon enough."

Mrs. Uffington flinched. "Why, I should perish in an instant! I've told you, I trust no one but you to give me my medications—not even myself!"

Lep placed to her lips a spoonful of green syrup, which she swallowed without hesitation. She then cheerfully gave up twelve ounces of blood, after which Lep deposited a pill down her throat, coasted downstairs to look in on Isaac, and discovered Dr. Peale in the room.

The doctor's eyes were fixed on the servant. "Isaac," he murmured, "has left us, I'm afraid."

Lep paled. He stared down at the black face sticking out from under a white vinegar-soaked sheet. Mrs. Uffington entered the room.

"He died," said Dr. Peale, "an hour ago." Perched next to the bed, long legged and stoop shouldered, he gazed down like a wading bird contemplating the water.

"*Died?*" erupted Mrs. Uffington. She strode forward and eyed Isaac in disbelief, as if she'd been promised by his previous employer that the boy would live forever. "You're certain the scoundrel's not simply pretending?"

"Quite certain," Dr. Peale replied.

In disgust, Mrs. Uffington shook her head, as though Isaac had committed a great disloyalty. "Unfortunately, with the outside air swimming with noxious effluvia, it's not enough to be proof against the fever alone."

Dr. Peale lifted his head. "But madam, the Negroes—"

"He might have inhaled any of a dozen distempers." Mrs. Uffington glanced at Lep. "Though had you alone tended him, he'd no doubt be alive today." She scowled at the serving boy. "And working!"

She turned about and swept out of the room, leaving Lep standing beside his master.

"I made use of every means of cure I could think of," Dr. Peale mused.

Lep swallowed. "Most likely he was treated too late."

"Not just Isaac." Dr. Peale faced his apprentice. "I'm speaking, Asclepius, of all the patients I've attempted to aid—so many of whom have died."

Lep had never seen the man in such a state and longed to bolster his flagging spirits.

"But people are streaming back into the city," the apprentice asserted. "The fever is conquered."

"It's the frost that's halted it, as it's known to do, rather than our medications, I'm afraid."

Lep was transfixed by this statement. In wonder, he peered at Dr. Peale. Did he realize what it was he was saying?

Lep swallowed. "But what of Mrs. Uffington—and the others?"

"It pains me to say," Dr. Peale replied, "that they

stand in the minority—and seem to have recovered not because of our remedies but rather in spite of them."

Lep was struck speechless. In disbelief, he eyed his master. Was he renouncing everything he'd taught to Lep?

" *'Primum non nocere'* is, as you know, the first rule of medicine," said Dr. Peale.

" 'First of all, do no harm,' " Lep translated.

"Exactly. And in the case of the yellow fever, it may be that that's *all* we're able to do."

Lep felt as if the sky was falling in the streets. The floor seemed to shift, the walls to sway.

"But surely," he pleaded, "the bark is potent—and the other medications you've prescribed."

Dr. Peale breathed deeply. "With other ills, perhaps. But this sickness mocks all medicine. Indeed, it may be that the only effective remedy we have to offer is faith."

"Faith?" Lep peered at his master, bewildered.

Dr. Peale walked slowly up to a window. "In 1625, at the siege of Breda, it's said that the Prince of Orange used it to rid an entire garrison of scurvy." He gazed through the glass as if beholding the scene. "He mixed up a worthless concoction of wormwood and water and declared it a wondrous medicine, procured with the greatest difficulty from the East. A medicine so strong he would not allow more than a single drop to be given each man." He paused. "Eagerly, the men took their doses." Dr. Peale turned around toward Lep. "And were cured."

He approached the apprentice. "Faith is a drug of great powers, relied on by every physician. A drug whose dispensing I've never had need to instruct you in, as you've mastered its use."

Lep was indignant at being charged with such deception. "How is that?"

"Without knowing," said the doctor. "You've a way of imparting hope to your patients, through your confidence in your cures. And you possess the gift of inspiring great trust—a talent that resides, I believe, in your eyes."

"My eyes?" Lep felt a surge of loyalty to the remedies he'd applied and refused to believe his eyes were of any import. "Our patients who survived were cured by *faith*?"

"In part, perhaps," Dr. Peale replied. "Just why they recovered remains a mystery." He slapped the toe of his shoe on a bedbug. "It's a grave vanity to believe ourselves omniscient."

Lep gaped at his master, stunned by his loss of faith in the sovereignty of medicine. Had his mind been unbalanced by Isaac's death? Had his belief in his cures always been frail? Lep felt as if the planets had gone whirling out of their accustomed orbits. Had he, like Clara, been serving a pretender?

Dr. Peale viewed a passing wagon through the window. "We'll head home once we locate Clara. But it will not be a victory march, I'm afraid." He rested his gaze on Isaac's body. "But rather, a time to meditate on the flaws in our knowledge—and the feebleness of our powers."

Lep gawked at the doctor, thunderstruck by such heresy. He'd been abandoned, betrayed by the very man he'd respected above all others. He felt desolate, as if he'd been orphaned—then abruptly he drew back from Dr. Peale.

He was a turncoat, Lep told himself, a traitor to medicine, no better than all the rest who'd thronged to religion or quackery. Lep had been fooled by him, had even yearned to please him—but the fever had brought out his infamy. No doubt he hoped his apprentice would defect as well—but he was wrong! Lep felt suddenly armored with resolve. His master might disown his drugs and potions—but *never* would Lep lay down his arms!

He turned and stalked out of the room, retrieved his chest, and set off on his rounds alone.

"Nothing to offer but faith!" he hissed, mocking his master's words. He drew to a halt before a shop window and viewed his large brown eyes in the reflection. Wishing he could exchange them for a different pair, small as a spider's and drab as ditchwater, he scoffed at their powers and strode ahead down the sidewalk. Feeling himself the standard-bearer of his profession, he proudly tended to his patients, heroically battling the fever on their behalf, driving from his mind the thought that Dr. Peale might be right and his labors in vain.

At sunset he headed toward Mr. Tweakfield's, still staggered by his mentor's revelation. The November air was unusually mild. He met two stray dogs, their ribs protruding, who sniffed him hopefully as he passed. He encountered a family all smoking cigars and another stepping carefully down the center of the street so as to avoid any contact with the houses of the sick.

Arriving at Mr. Tweakfield's, Lep found Marcus and Mary just serving supper. He eyed the pair suspiciously, wondering why they were trying to turn their master against him. Then he noticed the fire in the dining room hearth.

"Odd to have a fire," the apprentice remarked, "with the air so summery outside."

Marcus smiled at the apprentice and set a bowl of quinces on the table. "Mr. Tweakfield ordered the blaze set himself."

At that, Mr. Tweakfield entered the room, took a pinch of snuff, and sat down. The apprentice began eating, then noticed that his host was wearing a fur-trimmed coat. Lep reached for a quince, glanced at the man's face, and found it paler than usual. Then he dropped his knife, leaned forward in his chair, spied a pair of red marks on Mr. Tweakfield's throat—and dashed at once for his medicine chest.

113

Chapter Nine

ESCAPE

Lep settled Mr. Tweakfield in his bedroom and bled him at once, hoping to halt the fever in its tracks. Watching the blood drain into the bowl, he scoffed at the notion that he had nothing to offer his patients but faith in worthless cures. Dr. Peale had renounced his own regimen, but Lep would remain faithful to it—and *prove* its potency by curing Mr. Tweakfield.

All night Lep remained at Mr. Tweakfield's side, mixing drugs, changing poultices, grappling desperately with the fever. He took note of the disease's every change of aspect, studying the body before him as if he were a general looking down on a field of battle— and found his eyes drawn to the patient's scar, and his thoughts to the battle of Stony Point. That skirmish, he'd been told, had been very brief, yet the sound of the fray had filled Lep's ears without stop ever since he'd spied the spots on Mr. Tweakfield's throat. And by tending the man who'd fought beside his father, he felt as if, at last, he was able to reach his hands back into the past and dress the wounds of the man whose plea for a doctor he'd been unable to answer.

Before sunrise Lep bled Mr. Tweakfield again. The man's eyes were bloodshot, his skin yellowish. His gums and nose had begun to bleed. Lep realized the disease was progressing quickly and recalled that some of those stricken had died in as little as twelve hours' time. Nevertheless, he'd arranged to meet Clara at the river. After administering a dose of bark, he promised his groggy patient that he'd return as quickly as he could, and departed.

At dawn he was standing on Pemberton's Wharf while the sun, hidden by the river's mist, snuck inconspicuously into the sky as if returning discreetly from a night of carousing.

The apprentice waited. The fog began to thin. Tiring, he sat down on the burlap sack he'd brought—then sprang up like a Jack-in-the-box. He heard the sound of oars parting the water. Boring into the mist like a beacon, he made out a figure in a boat. It was Clara.

"Lep?"

He waved his arms. "Over here."

Clara guided the skiff to the wharf, picked up her brother, and headed back the way she'd come.

"Did you get the fifty dollars?" he asked.

Clara nodded her head.

"And you hid the trunk?"

"At the stern, underneath an old sail."

Lep found himself fidgeting nervously, wishing he were safely back on the wharf. Recalling that neither of them could swim, he wondered if that was sufficient grounds for postponing the plan, or canceling it entirely—then he spied the *Angel of Mercy* and crawled under the burlap lest he be seen.

"I'll tie up to the rope ladder," Clara informed him.

Lep knew she must be just as fainthearted—but that she wouldn't deign to admit to the fact.

"Near the stern," she added. "On the starboard side."

Lep puckered his lips at such nautical terms. Then he realized she'd be bringing them home, tokens of her vast experience of the sea—and that there'd be no more rooting them out of her than washing the dapples off a horse.

The oars ceased to sound. Lep went stiff as a corpse, just in case Mr. Botkin should chance to be watching. Then the skiff banged up against something solid.

"I'll give you a signal," whispered Clara, "when it's safe to stand up and take hold of the trunk."

She climbed out of the skiff. Lep lay stone still, listening.

The current purred softly. A pair of birds squawked, far off. Gently, the skiff shifted about, nuzzling the larger boat like a calf.

Lep felt a mosquito nip his neck through the burlap and jerked, restraining himself from striking back. Another commenced to whine in his ear and he gritted his teeth, wondering where Clara was. She had only to speak a moment with Mr. Botkin, making certain that he was settled below. The apprentice endured another bite, trying to guess what sort of signal she'd give. He sharpened his ears, but heard only mosquitoes. Then all at once he felt bites three, four, and five—and flung off the sack, determined to get the trunk into the skiff by himself while his sister chattered away with Mr. Botkin.

He grabbed the rope ladder, put one toe on a rung, and listened for any trace of footsteps. Hearing nothing, he climbed up on the deck and spotted a lump under a rotting sail. He tiptoed up to it, soft footed as a cat. Peeling back the canvas, he beheld his father's trunk, bent down, and hoisted it onto his shoulder. Then he headed toward the skiff—and suddenly heard voices.

The apprentice froze. Then he spun around, wondering which direction to run, and finally scampered back toward the sail and put the trunk under the canvas again. Lifting his head, he heard no more talking. Hoping he had time to get back into the skiff, he crouched low as a chipmunk, lit out toward the ladder, caught one foot in a fold of the sail—and went sprawling across the deck just as Clara and Mr. Botkin appeared.

"Great heavens!" Mr. Botkin, his eye twitching

wildly, cautiously approached the apprentice.

"Clara! I do believe—it's your brother!" Astounded, Mr. Botkin peered at the boy, and seemed even more worried by the meeting than Lep.

"Yes, sir," stammered Clara. "He's come—for a visit."

Lep rose up. "We met by chance. At the wharf."

Mr. Botkin anxiously tugged at the tattered cuffs of his coat and cleared his throat. "I see. And is your mother—visiting as well?"

"No, sir!"

Mr. Botkin appeared to breathe easier. "Well now." He smiled warmly at Lep. "As I was just explaining to your sister here, I've a batch of my antipestilential rings just ready to be raised up out of the water."

He scuttled toward the stern on his stumpy legs, missing the trunk by no more than a foot, and pulled on a rope that led over the side.

"Rings of Egyptian iron, these are. Extremely costly—as no doubt you're aware. And now fully saturated with the electric fire."

Lep endeavored to appear impressed while Mr. Botkin hauled up a dripping pouch of finely woven netting, filled with black rings of various sizes.

"While others are lured by the siren song of riches or fame," he addressed the apprentice, "my own ears have ever and always been attuned to the voice of suffering mankind." He inspected the rings with satisfaction. "And you may report to your mother that, with

Clara's help, my mission of mercy has saved hundreds of souls. And that such profits as happen to accrue will go toward repaying her generous loan—and toward furthering the *rigorous* scientific researches that led me to the rings."

Lep struggled to smile. "I'll be certain to tell her."

"But at the moment," piped up Clara, hoping to shoo Mr. Botkin below, "there's much work to be done."

Mr. Botkin beamed in agreement, anxious to be rid of the boy. "Yes, indeed! Mighty labors—that many more might be saved!" Desperately untying the pouch, as if a dozen lives depended on his speed, he flew across the deck, fell over the trunk, picked himself up—and threw back the canvas.

"And what in God's garden is *this?*" he boomed.

Clara exchanged owllike glances with her brother.

"It's—my trunk," Lep sputtered. "I was just—bringing it aboard."

Mr. Botkin stared at it spitefully, rubbing his shin. "I'd have thought it was Clara's."

"The two are alike!" she spoke up suddenly.

"Both made by Mr. Diggs—in Danfield," offered Lep. He scurried forward toward the trunk. "But rather than disrupt your life-saving labors, I believe I'll stay elsewhere after all."

Clara climbed down into the skiff. "And you, sir, ought to return below, lest the rays of the sun infect you with the fever."

Mr. Botkin went pale. His eye took to twitching.

"The fever—from the rays of the sun?"

Lep spotted the rings on his fingers and was startled that the man should exhibit such fear.

"Yes, sir," declared Clara, recalling Lep's instructions. "It's been found out and proved—scientifically."

Mr. Botkin glanced skyward. "But the sun isn't shining!"

Quickly, Lep lifted the trunk to his shoulder, crossed the deck, and thrust it toward Clara with such force that it fell into the skiff, opened up—and discharged a noisily jingling petticoat.

Mr. Botkin looked down, then fixed his gaze on Lep. "And what would you be doing with a petticoat?"

Speechlessly, Lep stared down upon it. It was tied in a knot—and in horror he realized that the jingling had come from the fifty dollars that Clara had tied up inside it.

Mr. Botkin grabbed hold of the apprentice's arm. "Or might you be conniving to snatch her back home—and telling me twisters all along!"

Lep ransacked his wits for something to say. He felt the strength drain out of his limbs—and saw that Clara was untying the skiff.

"It's true!" he burst out, sweat streaming down his brow. "We've been lying to you all the while!"

Terror-stricken, Clara stared up at Lep.

"I didn't come to visit, but rather—to be cured."

"*Cured?*" Mr. Botkin quickly dropped Lep's arm.

"I've been here a week, tending the sick—and noticed the first signs of fever this morning."

Mr. Botkin took note of the sweat on his brow and backed away from Lep as from Death himself, displaying scant faith in the invincible protection of the pair of rings adorning his fingers.

"I convinced Clara to come and serve as my nurse. And hearing of the rings—I'd hoped they might help."

"Yes, yes! By all means! They're invincible aids!" Trembling, Mr. Botkin bent down, snatched up the pouch of rings, and flung it at Lep, sending the contents rolling about the deck.

"Take them, boy! Take them and begone!"

Fleeing for his life, the man disappeared—as did Lep, down the ladder and into the skiff. At once Clara commenced to beat the water with the oars as if stirring up batter, and had them at the wharf in ten minutes' time. Jealous of her competence at rowing, Lep manfully raised the trunk to his shoulder and led the way down the wharf.

"Do you suppose," asked Clara, "that he'll come after us once he finds the money gone?" She turned and sighted the *Angel of Mercy* through the mist.

"Let him try," Lep replied, secretly hoping Mr. Botkin wouldn't take his advice. "Just look how long it took me to find you." He cast a glance back at the boat. "And besides, he's too frightened of catching the fever. No *wonder* he moved to that boat of his—and was set on getting one of us for an assistant."

"But what will he do with all the rings left to sell?"

Lep noticed that Clara still had her basket. "I don't know what *he'll* do—but you can get rid of yours right here." Lep aimed his eyes at the water.

Clara stopped, then strolled toward the edge of the wharf.

"Including the pair on your fingers," Lep called out.

Clara removed the two bags from her basket and poured their rings into the river. Glancing at the two on her fingers, she slipped them off slowly, gazed down at the water—and quickly snuck them into a pocket, just in case there was something to them.

"You can wear this instead," said Lep, approaching. He set down the trunk and untied from his neck the bag of camphor Dr. Peale had given him. "As you'll be in contact with the sick, you'll be needing it."

He smiled at her ringless fingers, as if having cleansed an altar of foreign idols, and tied the bag around her neck with the air of one restoring the true faith.

"Then we're not leaving for home right away?" spoke up Clara.

"Not until Mr. Tweakfield recovers. I thought you could help me in tending him."

"Why, surely!" Clara replied, glad to be staying for any reason, determined to get full value from her chance to see the world beyond Danfield.

The mist burned off and their shadows appeared, preceding them down the streets. Arriving at Mr. Tweakfield's house, Lep introduced his sister, showed her to his room, and rushed to his patient's bedside.

Mr. Tweakfield's skin had become dry and hot. At once Lep began sponging him with vinegar—while Clara, alone in the bedroom, placed in the left and right pockets of her dress the rings she'd worn on her left and right fingers.

"Some broth for Mr. Tweakfield," announced Marcus, stepping in. He set down a bowl on the night table and smiled pleasantly at the apprentice. Lep, like a flawed mirror, refused to smile back, sure that he and Mary had cunningly placed the silver tray and spoons—in hopes that Mr. Tweakfield would turn him out of the house as a thief.

Clara entered and assisted sponging the patient. He was propped up in bed, his skin yellow in places and his eyelids heavy.

"You'll be pleased to know, sir," Marcus addressed him, "that I've distributed the porcelain punch bowl and cups among the poor, as you desired."

Lep looked at Clara, recalled the punch bowl, and put down his sponge, hardly believing his ears. Diligently over the past several days he'd read to Mr. Tweakfield of the experiments of Hauksbee, Galvani, and Gray, building what he'd thought was an impregnable fortification against the man's fears.

"Given to the needy in Almond Street," said Marcus. "Where this morning I shall take the table and chairs you specified."

Lep stared at the footman's ruddy face, then turned in dismay toward his patient.

"Thank you, Marcus," Mr. Tweakfield mumbled. Apologetically, he glanced at Lep.

"In addition," remarked the footman, "I thought you might be interested in seeing this." He reached a plump hand into his coat pocket and came out with a purple duck egg. Stepping close to Mr. Tweakfield, he rotated the egg before his master's eyes, displaying the black squiggles that covered the shell—and stopping at a spot where the markings had formed into letters, and the letters into words.

Mr. Tweakfield's eyelids shot up like flushed pheasant. The letters spelled CHRIST IS COMING.

"While absorbed in studying the Scriptures yesterday, Mary and I were suddenly aroused by an extraordinary squawking coming from Emma." Marcus entrusted the egg to Mr. Tweakfield, who viewed it and handed it fearfully to Clara.

"Your duck—laid *this?*" she asked, disbelieving. Having been shown up by Lep through her gullibility, she was determined to rebuild her reputation for worldly wisdom by doubting everything.

"Indeed." Marcus fixed a blissful smile on the egg. "She's but one of many prophets announcing the Day, when time will cease altogether, Gabriel's trumpet will sound in the sky, and the saved will be borne to heaven by the four winds." Suddenly his smile vanished. "Yet a day that will burn like an oven for the wicked. When the Lord shall reap the stalk of the earth and cast the sinful into the everlasting fire."

Clara snorted. She passed the egg to Lep and from the window spied Emma nosing weeds below.

"A duck—the spokesman for God?" she inquired.

Marcus grinned. "The Lord speaks through all his creations. Through the falling stars, the plague of mosquitoes. And through the pestilence as well. For the fever is nothing other than His sickle and we in Philadelphia His sharpening stone, upon which He hones it for the harvest to come." He turned his gaze toward Mr. Tweakfield. "And last evening, when I raised my head from my prayers, I beheld in the sky still another herald of the Day—the northern lights."

Lep studied the egg suspiciously, then returned it to the footman. "I was here all night, with the curtains parted, and never saw any sign of them."

Marcus smiled indulgently at the apprentice. "They come and go quickly, as everyone knows. But their message is perfectly clear just the same." He set the egg on Mr. Tweakfield's table, with the words facing toward him, and left the room.

Lep cleaned the blood from Mr. Tweakfield's nose.

"Excuse me, sir," the apprentice said softly. "But are you not depriving your rightful heirs by giving away your possessions?"

The patient licked at his lips, his teeth dark from the doses of mercury he'd been given. "I've a sister, likewise unmarried. In Peckford. Two days west of Danfield." He turned his head, with difficulty, toward Lep. "But I've only cast off a few trifles, believe me. Just in case—" He eyed the egg beside him.

Lep picked up Galvani's *Commentary on the Effect of Electricity on Muscular Motion.* Placing it next to the egg, he left Clara to feed Mr. Tweakfield his broth and departed to attend to Mrs. Uffington.

Carts and coaches rumbled through the streets, bearing their occupants back to their homes. Lep saw windows thrown open to air out houses and smelled rooms being cleansed with brimstone smoke. Walls were being whitewashed, clothing baked in ovens, and carpets drenched with vinegar.

Stepping inside, Lep administered to Mrs. Uffington her final treatment and declared her recovered. Finding Dr. Peale in the parlor, Lep curtly informed him that Clara had been found and that Mr. Tweakfield had taken ill with the fever.

Dr. Peale shook his head sympathetically. Bitterly, Lep regarded the man, sure he expected Mr. Tweakfield to die. Vowing to disprove him, Lep stalked outside, bound for his few remaining patients.

Two hours later he headed back toward Mr. Tweakfield's. He passed a bill advertising the services of a woman much experienced with the fever in Charleston and possessing a miraculous powder to combat it. Lep eyed the paper scornfully, proud to have separated Clara from such quackery. Glancing about for Mr. Botkin, he wondered if he and Clara were as safe from the man as he'd so bravely made out. The rogue might be powerfully afraid of the fever—but the lure of money might be too strong to resist. Alert for any sign of him, Lep walked on, turned a corner, then spotted a pair of white horses—and stopped in his tracks.

They were hitched to a cart that was drawn up beside a shed. Lep studied them from across the street and was certain he recognized them as Mr. Tweakfield's. Wondering what they were doing there, he walked over to the shed, looked in a window—and felt the blood commence to race through his veins.

On a table he sighted the porcelain punch bowl and cups that Mr. Tweakfield had relinquished—and that Marcus had said he'd already given away to the needy in Almond Street. Lep recalled treating a patient on that very street—and knew it was many blocks to the south. Glancing to his left, he saw a stack of Mr. Tweakfield's books of law and the clothing Marcus and Mary had cast off—and all at once he knew for certain that their piety was a sham. They'd just *stored* what they'd claimed to have handed out to the poor, and had tried to get rid of him for fear his reading aloud might convince Mr. Tweakfield not to give up his possessions—

possessions they meant to make off with themselves! Lep dashed up to the cart. It held a table and chairs. Just then footsteps sounded. He whirled around, and found himself face to face with Marcus.

Chapter Ten

JUDGMENT DAY

Marcus froze. Stupefied, he stared at Lep and licked at his twisted upper lip. Then his face contorted as if he'd been struck by lightning and his features jerked into a smile.

"Why, Lep," he purred. "What an unexpected pleasure."

Lep's tongue felt as if it had been cast in lead. Wondering if Marcus had seen him at the window—and what action the man might take if he had—Lep glanced at the burly footman, then at the shuttered windows of the house beside the shed.

"As you know, Mr. Canby, who's on business in England, engaged me to watch over his property." Marcus quickly closed the shed door, secured it with a padlock, and dropped the key in his pocket. "A chore

I thought I'd attend to before proceeding on to Almond Street."

"I see," Lep replied, anxious to be gone.

Marcus climbed up into the cart. "The destitute are *quite* numerous there." The footman gazed feelingly at Lep. "However, with Mr. Tweakfield's help, many will be able to pay off their debts—and be summoned to the Judgment with spotless souls."

He smiled at the thought and took up the reins.

"Yes, of course!" Lep spoke up. "And I'd best be off also." He picked up his medicine chest and set out while the cart clattered off in the opposite direction. Frantic to tell Mr. Tweakfield what he'd seen, he sped through the streets and charged through the door.

"Lep!" Clara streaked up to him as he entered, glanced about, and yanked him into the library.

"I decided to study Emma for myself and was following her around the yard—when I spotted these on the port side of her pen."

Lep rolled his eyes at her nautical talk, then watched as she opened her palm and revealed a handful of eggshells, gold on one side. The pieces were covered with wormy black squiggles. On the largest piece appeared the letters TRU, the U of which had been marred by a thumbprint.

"The letters look exactly the same as those on the other egg," whispered Clara.

Lep licked a finger and rubbed it against the shell. The gold coloring began to fade.

"It's just dye!" he gasped. "And the lettering's ink—put on no doubt by Mr. Tweakfield's servants!"

Clara trained a triumphantly skeptical eye on the shells. "Emma! A prophet!"

Bursting with desire to proclaim his discoveries, Lep dashed up the stairs ahead of Clara—and was stopped dead in Mr. Tweakfield's doorway by the sight of Mary hunched over the man.

"What's that in your hands?" the apprentice demanded.

Mary turned. "Another egg," she answered in her solemn monotone. "Produced just moments ago by Emma, and containing a wondrous communication."

Lep hurried forward and snatched the egg from her fingers. It was gold, with black squiggles that had formed into letters—spelling GABREIL'S TRUMPET SOUNDS AT DAWN.

Lep gawked at the egg, then peered down at his patient. "It's not Emma at all!" he shouted out. "The words have been written on the egg—by your servants!"

Mary's birchbark skin whitened further. Slowly Mr. Tweakfield licked his lips, staring out blankly from beneath his heavy eyelids.

"Just look!" Clara cried, thrusting the piece of shell with TRU into his view. "I found it in the weeds by Emma's pen. The same color, the same handwriting, the same letters as the egg—and with the mark of a thumb on the 'u'!"

Mary eyed the shell in surprise. "It appears," she addressed Mr. Tweakfield, "that Emma's found a new spot to lay. No doubt the egg escaped our attention."

"Escaped?" Lep exclaimed. "On the contrary, you hid it there yourselves after smudging it—knowing the thumbprint would betray the fact that the writing was put on by human hands."

Mary smiled. "A laughable tale."

Mr. Tweakfield gazed vaguely at the piece of shell.

"The eggs have been dyed!" Lep appealed to his patient, demonstrating the fact before his eyes. "Then simply scribbled on with ink!"

"And by someone who couldn't spell!" declared Clara. She exhibited Mary's egg to Mr. Tweakfield. "Unless you believe the Almighty himself would mix up the 'i' and the 'e' in 'Gabriel'!"

In terror, Mary stared at the egg, focusing on the archangel's name. Proudly, Lep grinned at his sister, having failed to spot the mistake before.

"The nearness of the Day," Mary faltered, "has unbalanced their youthful minds, I'm afraid." She bent closer to her oblivious master. "The coming Judgment has thrown them into a panic—with good reason, as just this morning I discovered that the girl, with her brother's taste for thieving, had hidden four of your silver snuffboxes underneath her pillow."

Clara stared openmouthed at the woman. "Lies!" she hissed. "Why, you should hang from the yardarm!"

"And it's *them* who've been thieving!" Lep cried out.

He grasped one of Mr. Tweakfield's hands, as if hoping to impart the truth by touch. "They've been trying to scare you out of your possessions and have *kept* all they claim to have showered on the poor—in a shed, over on Sassafras Street!"

Mary and Clara both viewed Lep in amazement.

"Naturally, sir," Mary spoke up loudly into Mr. Tweakfield's ear, "you won't let yourself be swayed by these children."

Clara aimed an outraged glance at the woman.

"Strive to ignore their meaningless babble and concentrate instead on the Day—which arrives in but a few short hours."

Mr. Tweakfield's eyes had closed completely. Seeing that it was useless to speak further, Mary glided out of the room. At once, while Clara fetched their belongings, Lep snatched a loaf of bread from the kitchen, returned to Mr. Tweakfield's room behind his sister— and hurriedly locked the door. He didn't intend to give Marcus and Mary another chance to cheat their master. And now that he'd revealed the secret of the shed, he'd feel better knowing that he and Clara were safe from the servants as well. Until, that is, Mr. Tweakfield revived, learned the truth, and dismissed the rogues.

Lep counted the strokes of his patient's pulse and found his skin still hot and dry. Ignoring Dr. Peale's doubts, he drew out twenty-five ounces of blood, administered ten grains of opium, and sponged the man's face with cool vinegar. Glancing at the table beside the bed, he picked up the egg that proclaimed CHRIST IS COMING and tossed it into the chamber pot. Clara, still fuming at being called a child, did the same for the egg announcing Gabriel's trumpet.

The sun went down. The stars emerged, cautiously, as if from hiding. Faithfully, Lep read to Mr. Tweak-field, in hopes that it might infuse him with strength, and to let him know that he'd not been abandoned. Long after midnight, when the sky was tenanted by unfamiliar constellations, the apprentice at last blew out his light.

Suddenly Clara was shaking him as if she meant to rearrange his skeleton.

"Lep! Come to the window—quick!"

He opened his eyes, confused. It was dawn. He heard a great noise, and drowsily wondered whether it could actually be Gabriel's trumpet. Springing up, he lunged toward the window, looked down—and discovered instead that it was the sound of Mr. Tweakfield's cart charging into the street, piled with boxes and tables and chairs and driven by none other than Marcus and Mary.

Lep stood paralyzed.

"Come on!" cried Clara, shaking him by the shoulder. "We've got to catch them!"

Scrambling into their shoes, they scurried downstairs and looked about them in awe. Most of the furniture had vanished, along with the silver serving ware.

They dashed out the door and took off up the street. The cart was no longer in sight, and Lep feared they'd never get another glimpse of it. The servants must have turned. And suddenly he knew where—toward the shed, to retrieve their own belongings and the rest of Mr. Tweakfield's.

They rounded the corner, their shadows stretched out like taffy by the rising sun. Flying along, they passed a black man lifting a body into a coffin. Clara shoved her hands in her pockets and clutched her rings for protection. Then she stopped.

"A watchman!" she shouted to Lep. "Down the alley!"

"Bring him to Sassafras and Third," he called back, and continued on down the street. He turned another corner, sprinting full speed, and felt himself becoming winded. His stride shortened, his legs seemed to grow heavy. He looked ahead—then ducked behind an elm tree. The cart was parked half a block away.

Lep peeked around the trunk of the tree and saw Marcus and Mary carrying a table together from the shed to the cart. The apprentice wondered if he should wait for the watchman—then realized that the servants might slip away before the man arrived. Like a turtle he warily stuck out his head, and caught sight of the pair entering the shed. Quickly, he spurted ahead, then halted behind a hedge across the street from the cart. He peered between the branches and saw the servants appear, each with a pair of chairs. Knowing they couldn't have much more to load, he racked his brain for a way to stop them—then spotted the open padlock on the shed door.

Marcus climbed up onto the cart. He wedged in his chairs, then piled on Mary's. Lep swallowed. He watched them return to the shed—then burst from the hedge and sped across the street, slammed the door shut, and secured it with the lock.

There was pounding on the door—and in the street as well, as Clara and a portly, panting watchman trotted up to Lep.

"They're inside!" he cried, and proceeded to explain the servants' scheme to the watchman. Turning the rusty key in the lock, the watchman opened the door.

Marcus gaped at what he saw, then flashed a grateful smile. "Good sir, how fortunate you've arrived, before these devious children had a chance—"

"Keep quiet, you son of a serpent." The watchman handcuffed the servants together. "I spied Mr. Tweakfield's horses meself, haulin' a houseful of goods at a gallop, and suspicioned that something might not be right."

Marcus beamed at the man. "Dear sir—"

"And you can leave off grinnin' like a baked possum as well."

He led the pair down the street toward the jail, while Lep and Clara looked on with relief.

"The end of time!" scoffed Clara. "At dawn!" She

smiled smugly at the amber sun rising serenely into the sky.

"Yet Emma was right after all," said Lep.

Clara spun about toward her brother in shock.

"About Judgment Day arriving today," he added hastily. "For Marcus and Mary."

They retrieved what still remained in the shed and drove the cart to Mr. Tweakfield's. Together they began unloading it—until Lep realized that in the morning's turmoil he'd not even taken note of his patient.

He rushed upstairs and into the man's room. Mr. Tweakfield's eyes were open but it appeared that he was still wrapped in a stupor. Lep had hoped it would have lifted by now and permitted him the pleasure of revealing the facts about Marcus and Mary. He pulled a chair close and studied his patient. His skin was blazing hot, his pulse weak. His thundercloud eyebrows hung above yellow eyes that glistened strangely. Fending off Dr. Peale's confession, Lep opened up his medicine chest.

He mixed up an ointment to stimulate the liver, privately mocking his master's words and dismissing the powers said to reside in his eyes. Perhaps the hysterical Mrs. Uffington had been cured, in part, by faith—but Mr. Tweakfield was free of her delusions and would serve as the true test of medicine's potency. Even if every other doctor on earth joined Dr. Peale in surrendering to the fever, Lep vowed to remain true to the tools of his profession, and to prove to them all the dominion that drugs held over all disease.

He rubbed in the ointment, removed more blood, and breathing through a vinegar-soaked cloth, applied mustard plasters to draw out the heat. Undoubtedly, he mused, many who'd died had simply been treated too late in the illness. Most had lacked nurses to attend to them. Others had refused the benefits of medicine and had perished out of faith in sniffing tar, keeping garlic in their pockets, and other worthless remedies.

Confident his patient would soon revive, Lep finished emptying the cart with Clara, returning the furniture to its accustomed sites, restoring the silver platters to their shelves, setting the candlesticks back on the mantel. Then he climbed the stairs—and found Mr. Tweakfield writhing about in convulsions.

At once Lep administered a strong dose of bark. He attempted to sponge the man's face with cold water while Mr. Tweakfield, mumbling nonsensically, thrashed about like a fish on dry land. He'd never behaved in such a way before, and Lep realized in alarm that the disease had entered a different stage. The black vomit, the nosebleeds, the spells of great sweating appeared to be behind him. Lep trembled to think what might lie ahead.

By noon Mr. Tweakfield was lying still. Lep, however, was even more concerned. The man's pulse was now much fainter than before. His tongue was brown, his skin yellow as parchment. The apprentice applied the remedies usual for this stage and picked up Benjamin Franklin's *Experiments and Observations on Electricity*.

He began to read, uncertain whether Mr. Tweakfield could even hear him, striving as much to strengthen his own faith in science and medicine as to bolster his patient. Refusing to leave Mr. Tweakfield's side, he read aloud all afternoon, while the guns of Stony Point sounded in his head.

At dusk Clara entered with fruit and broth. Lep failed to get Mr. Tweakfield to eat. Driving his master's words from his mind, he meticulously mixed a fresh mustard plaster and applied it to Mr. Tweakfield's chest. Girded with lancet and bowl, he then drew off precisely twenty ounces of blood.

Lep threw open the windows to let in fresh air. He saw that Mr. Tweakfield's face had a purplish cast and found that his pulse had faded still further. Restless, having followed his regimen to the letter, knowing nothing else he could do for his patient, he quickly snatched up the book off the table. Finding the line at which he'd stopped, he resumed his reading, louder than before, hurriedly turning the pages as if the slightest pause in his voice might allow Mr. Tweakfield's life to lapse. The moon rose, unnoticed by Lep. Submerging himself entirely in his task, unaware of his voice carrying far down the street, he read on desperately for hours, growing hoarse, then feeling his voice disappearing—and suddenly stilled his tongue upon discovering that Mr. Tweakfield was dead.

Lep whirled about toward his medicine chest. Then, slowly, the apprentice uncoiled.

Lep swallowed. Dazed, he stared down at Mr. Tweakfield. The regimen had failed.

A breeze rustled the curtains and brushed Lep's cheek. He raised his eyes and glanced about. The room appeared different. The whole world seemed changed, a suddenly mysterious realm, only dimly comprehended.

Far into the night he stood beside the bed, while the guns of Stony Point faded in his ears.

Dr. Peale was right, he numbly reflected. The yellow fever still remained to be vanquished.

And Mr. Tweakfield, like his own father, was beyond saving. Even for someone named Asclepius.

In the morning Lep saw that the man was buried. He wrote a letter to Mr. Tweakfield's sister, arranged for Emma and the horses to be fed, packed his belongings in Clara's trunk, and set out with her toward Mrs. Uffington's.

Closemouthed, they walked through the streets, glancing at the returning families.

"Seems like everyone's going home," said Clara. She sighed, resigning herself to this fate, then noticed a knot of children ahead. She and Lep passed beside them, spied a body sprawled out on the ground—and stopped. It was Mr. Botkin.

He was dead, of the fever. In awe, they stared down

at him. He'd endeavored to protect himself by fitting as many of his rings as he could on his fingers. Around his neck he'd tied a rag dipped in tar. From one pocket a great head of garlic had fallen. From another, a bottle of Daffey's Elixir. Beside him, its mouth gaping open, lay a sack of his wonder-working rings.

Thunderstruck, Clara gawked at the man. His fingers were covered with the electrical rings—positive on the left hand, negative on the right. And yet—her eyes traveled to his purplish face, over which a pair of flies was crawling. He'd *lied* to her about the rings, she realized. And *she'd* lied to all those she'd sold them to.

Staggered, she glared venomously at the man. Then she whirled around and marched off down the sidewalk.

"Electrical rings!" Lep sneered in disgust.

Clara reached into the pockets of her dress, felt her own pair, and ground her teeth. She saw Lep turn for a last look at Mr. Botkin—and stealthily plucked the rings out and tossed them into a clump of weeds.

"Electrical rings, indeed!" she declared.

They reached Mrs. Uffington's and doused themselves with vinegar for what Lep hoped was the last time.

"Ready to depart, I see," said Dr. Peale, striding toward them down the hall. "No doubt your Mr. Tweakfield is fully recovered."

Lep swallowed, grateful he hadn't expressed his

short-lived contempt for his master.

"Mr. Tweakfield died last night," he answered.

Dr. Peale reached out and put a hand on Lep's shoulder just as Mrs. Uffington descended the stairs.

"You can't all be leaving me!" she gasped. "Why, who'll be left to do the work of the house?"

Dr. Peale looked up into her yellowish face. "You appear well able to care for yourself."

Lep smiled to himself at the words.

"Though most likely," continued Dr. Peale, "your family's on its way this very moment."

"Indeed they are—back to where they've been!" Mrs. Uffington glanced sourly at the front door. "They showed up yesterday—and took one look at the color of my face and fled quick as if the house were afire!" Mrs. Uffington snorted. "The moths I saw apparently held the souls of some *other* family." She gazed down proudly at her white attire. "But should the *right* moths appear, I'll not dress in black. And they can flutter all night at the window, pleading—but I'll never let them back in!"

Dr. Peale sighed at the persistence of her beliefs and collected his belongings by the door.

"You've a fine young helper," Mrs. Uffington addressed him, turning her eyes on Lep. "Possessed of great powers of healing, he is." She smiled at the apprentice, then turned toward Clara. "Why, without him I should have perished for certain."

Lep avoided her smile and endured her praise, thinking of his failure to save Mr. Tweakfield. Struck by the unfathomed mysteries of disease, he moved impatiently toward the door, anxious to be home and to continue poring over Dr. Peale's medical books—and, perhaps, to someday earn Mrs. Uffington's belief in his healing powers.

The three loaded their things into the gig, squeezed onto the seat, and bid farewell to Mrs. Uffington. Dr. Peale shook Hitabel's reins and they were off, Clara storing up a last look at the city while Lep, his devotion to his master renewed, eagerly studied his Latin primer.

"We did what we could," Dr. Peale spoke up, viewing the streets in which they'd battled the fever. He turned toward Lep. "And Mrs. Uffington was correct."

He cast a glance at Lep's Latin book.

"Discipulus bonus habeo," he stated, indicating that he had an excellent pupil.

Lep looked up into his master's eyes.

"Magister bonus habeo," he replied.

NOTE

More than 4,000 Philadelphians died during the yellow fever epidemic of 1793, nearly one tenth of the city's population. Unappeased, the disease returned in 1794, 1796, 1797, 1798, and for many years thereafter. It was not until 1902, in Panama, that Walter Reed discovered that yellow fever is not contagious and that its decline after cold weather and the red bumps on its victims are due to the fact that it's spread by those creatures the Philadelphia doctors all noted but never suspected—the mosquitoes.

About the Author

PAUL FLEISCHMAN *was born in Monterey, California, and grew up in Santa Monica. He attended the University of California at Berkeley and the University of New Mexico in Albuquerque, where he now makes his home. He is the author of three other books for children,* THE BIRTHDAY TREE, THE HALF-A-MOON INN, *and* GRAVEN IMAGES.